# *10 years of*
# HEARTBEAT

## A CELEBRATION OF HEARTBEAT: THE COUNTRYSIDE AND THE PEOPLE

Geoff Tibballs started his writing career as a journalist on the *Watford Observer*. A former press officer for ATV/Central Television he is the author of many books on television series including *London's Burning, Brookside, Soldier, Soldier* and *Cold Feet*. He is also the author of Carlton's bestselling book, *Titanic*. He lives in Nottingham.

# Acknowledgements

The author would like to thank the following for their
kind help in the preparation of this book:

Yorkshire Television's Controller of Drama, Keith Richardson

Kathryn de Belle and Philip Meeks at YTV

Nicky Paris, Gillian Holmes, Susanna Wadeson
and Roseanne Boyle at Granada Media.

First published in Great Britain in 2002
by Granada Media, an imprint of André Deutsch Limited
20 Mortimer Street
London W1V 5HA

In association with Granada Media Group
Text copyright © Granada Media Group Ltd 2002
Heartbeat is a Yorkshire TV Production for ITV1

Photographs copyright © Granada Media Group Ltd
Except pgs 20–21, 29, 114–115 © Michael Busselle/Corbis Images

Managing Art Director: Jeremy Southgate
Project Editor: Gillian Holmes
Editorial Manager: Nicky Paris
Design: DW Design

ISBN 0 233 05045 0

Printed and bound in Italy

2 4 6 8 10 9 7 5 3 1

# *10 years of* HEARTBEAT

**A CELEBRATION OF HEARTBEAT: THE COUNTRYSIDE AND THE PEOPLE**

GRANADA

# Contents

# Introduction

## by **Keith Richardson**

On Friday 10 April 1992, Yorkshire Television launched a new drama series set in the 1960s starring Nick Berry, formerly of *EastEnders*, and based on the little-known 'Constable' books by Nicholas Rhea, the pen name of a former policeman, Peter Walker. The heart-warming stories of the North Yorkshire bobby and his doctor wife Kate (played by Niamh Cusack) became hugely popular, especially when the programme was switched to 8 p.m. on Sunday evenings, while the accompanying sixties music struck a definite chord with viewers. Ten years on, *Heartbeat* remains ITV's highest-rating drama series and shows no sign of flagging. Yet Yorkshire Television had originally bought the rights to the 'Constable' books back in the late 1970s, leaving them to gather dust for over a decade. 'If we'd done *Heartbeat* back in the seventies,' says the show's executive producer, Keith Richardson, who is also the Controller of Drama for Yorkshire Television, 'it would probably only have lasted a series simply because *All Creatures Great and Small* was covering similar territory. But, when we came along in 1992, we were seen as a refreshing change from some of the gritty dramas that set out to shock, and I think that's still the case. It was a brave decision for us to create a show where the central characters – Nick and Kate – were happy because usually to create the drama you need a couple who are constantly rowing. But we bucked the trend and people liked that.

'I think the show works for a number of reasons: the relationships, the ensemble feel, the good storytelling, the countryside, the music. At first some older viewers found it a bit odd that people drove across the moors to the sound of heavy rock music, but most of the feedback to the musical accompaniment was positive and it has proved one of the show's great strengths. Yet originally it was just included in the background on the radio as an attempt to remind people that it was a period piece because the village of Goathland – which plays our fictional Aidensfield – is two hundred years old, so there's no real feel of the sixties to it.

'A lot of *Heartbeat*'s success is due to the fact that it hasn't changed much over the ten years,' Richardson continues. 'And I have fought to keep it exactly the same while making it appear fresh. It's a tribute to the strength of the ensemble of actors that the show has survived so many cast changes. There is no one star. They are all excellent. For example, William

Simons as Ventress sometimes doesn't do much, but he makes the most of it and is so authentic. Whenever you hear that somebody in the cast wants to leave it's a nightmare. You think: How will we get over this? But in many respects it forces you to refresh the show.

'Each week we have a crime and a humorous strand and for years Bill Maynard as Greengrass was terrific in the humorous strand; but Greengrass's successor, Vernon Scripps [Bernie Scripps's half-brother] has worked really well and has formed a great team with Bernie and David. In the most recent series [the eleventh] when Philip Franks [who played Craddock] wanted to go, we were able to replace him with a new sergeant, Merton, who is a much darker character. Whereas the previous station sergeants – Blaketon and Craddock – always got the wrong person, leaving Nick or Mike to solve the crime, Merton is a bit sharper. So it has given us a different angle.

'When Niamh Cusack left because she was pregnant in real life, our options were limited. I couldn't believe that Kate would have left Nick for another man because their relationship was so strong. We toyed with the idea of her reluctantly following her career in London, but that didn't seem right, so in the end she had to die. But it gave us our highest ratings and we were able to give her a heroine's death. There's no point in killing off characters unless the viewers really like them. That storyline was one where the music worked extremely well. When Kate was in a coma Nick got into bed beside her. The next thing you saw was him opening the curtains with the clear indication that something had happened. The music was Cat Stevens's "How Can I Tell You I Love You", and then you suddenly realised that Nick had spent all night cuddling her before she had died. It was pretty emotional stuff.

'Another of my favourite episodes was the foot-and-mouth story from Series Two. Nick Berry had a lot of reacting rather than acting to do in that. He wasn't dressed in the best way to be a star – in his sou'wester he looked a bit like Paddington Bear – but I thought he was terrific. You could feel his genuine concern for the farmer. We used music well in that story, too, with the orchestral version of "Nights In White Satin" playing in the background. What I feel personally vindicated about is that a lot of people laughed at the scene of the cows being burned and you saw one with its legs in the air on top of the pyre. But the images on the news last year were exactly what we showed.

'Originally we shot everything on location, but once we realised the show was going to run we thought it was worth building interior sets, partly to stop interfering with people's businesses in Goathland. Our first sets were the police station and Aidensfield Arms interiors at an Otley industrial unit, but, when *Emmerdale* left their Farsley Mill studios on the outskirts of Leeds, we moved there. We still film regularly in Goathland – usually three days per episode – but for our latest series we have been restricted by the foot-and-mouth disease. For instance we couldn't use Greengrass's farm for months. We were about to start filming a story about a bent auctioneer (played by John Nettles) when the epidemic broke. The story should have been livestock but we had to change it to farm machinery. But I think it's fair to say we've been good for the economy of Goathland. We've certainly put it on the tourist map.

'Some people say the crime level in Aidensfield is higher than Chicago, but my favourite review said that we revisited the sixties with Stalinist zeal, meaning we cut out all the unpleasant bits. But things were very different then.

'Heartbeat is a series which has genuine warmth. Some critics think it's very soft and gentle, but actually it's quite tough. However, we quite deliberately tell the stories so as not to upset or alienate our viewers. I remember one director saying to me, "I don't understand this story. Why does a man go out with a shotgun and hold up a lorry loaded with old slippers?" I said, "Because, when he set out to rob it, he didn't know it was full of old slippers!" To me, that sort of quirky approach to crime sums up what *Heartbeat* is all about. We tell good stories, we tell them well; people know what they're going to get. And I'm not ashamed of that.'

# chapter 1

# *The Rowans Move North*

The sixties came slowly to Aidensfield. Where London was swinging, this corner of rural North Yorkshire swayed gently. Fashions remained firmly entrenched in the fifties.  As for the newfangled pop music, many homes didn't get much racier than David Whitfield.

Claude Jeremiah Greengrass – Aidensfield's one-man crime wave.

## Heroes and Villains

Crime in the Ashfordly of the sixties was mercifully free of the ills that blighted city life at the time. Protection rackets, bank robberies and murders may have been commonplace in London, Liverpool and Leeds, but the trusty officers based at Ashfordly police station were more likely to be called out on cases of sheep worrying.

Their leader was Sergeant Oscar Blaketon, an old soldier who ran the station with military precision. Some said that his gruff exterior hid a heart of stone, but there was a more caring side

*'Right. Claude Jeremiah Greengrass. Mark the name well, Rowan. He's trouble. The type who thinks the law is there for others and not for him.'*
*– Blaketon*

to him, although this was generally concealed from his colleagues for fear of undermining his position. Ever since the departure of his wife, Blaketon had devoted his energies to work. He was a copper 24 hours a day and expected similar dedication in others. His senior officer, PC Alf Ventress, unfailingly fell short of those standards. Ventress was often described as being part of the furniture, if only because he was invariably no more animated than the average desk. A crisis to Ventress was a late lunch break. But he did have his uses and because he had been around since the Dark Ages he knew his community and had a photographic memory for people and places. Unfortunately, Ventress's slothlike ways were beginning to rub off on young PC Phil Bellamy, who at times appeared more interested in chasing girls than criminals.

Public Enemy Number One was Claude Jeremiah Greengrass, an old rogue who had his finger in more pies than Little Jack Horner.

> **Did you know?**
> Bill Maynard was once a footballer with Leicester City.

No-nonsense Sgt. Oscar Blaketon ran Ashfordly Police Station with military precision.

managed to stay one step ahead of the law. He lived on a rundown smallholding with his flea-ridden lurcher dog, Alfred – a natural deterrent to unwelcome visitors. It wasn't that Alfred would catch them: more a case of what they would catch from Alfred.

Greengrass knew he had the measure of the local boys, but the arrival of a new young PC from London presented a fresh challenge. Nick Rowan and his doctor wife Kate moved into the police house in Aidensfield after he decided to quit the Met in order to pursue his ideal of becoming a village bobby. Neither was a stranger to the area. Nick had been evacuated to the North York Moors as a boy during the war and Kate was born near Aidensfield before heading for London to study medicine.

Nick quickly crossed swords with Greengrass after Alfred broke into an aviary and killed a budgie. Blaketon demanded that Nick charge Greengrass with livestock worrying, but, when the case came to court, Greengrass pointed out to the magistrates that budgies are not classed as livestock under the Dogs (Protection of Livestock) Act of 1953. Furthermore, an aviary did not constitute agricultural land. As Blaketon silently seethed, the chairman of magistrates highlighted Rowan's inexperience of country matters and set Greengrass free. That night Nick and Kate returned home to find a dead hare hanging in their porch. It was someone's way of welcoming the couple to the area.

## Kate's crusade

Strictly a petty criminal, Greengrass was always on the lookout for ways of making easy money – which brought him into constant conflict with Blaketon, who was eager to pin anything from pheasant poaching to the Great Train Robbery on Greengrass. Indeed Blaketon had made it his life's mission to bring Greengrass to justice. But Greengrass was a wily character who somehow

While Nick soon integrated himself into village life, Kate battled to win over hearts and minds, particularly that of the local GP, Alex Ferrenby. Kate had been happy to leave her hospital job in London, partly because the long hours she worked there were putting a strain on her marriage and also because Ferrenby, her childhood mentor, had half promised her a job in Aidensfield. But Ferrenby belonged to the old school and now decided that Aidensfield wasn't ready for a woman doctor. They clashed again when Kate recommended that a struggling mother of six – Susan Maskell – should take the contraceptive pill to avoid any further unwanted pregnancies. Ferrenby had yet to come to terms with the moral and medical implications of the Pill and was initially outraged by the idea before Kate's powers of persuasion eventually won him round. However, the lull in hostilities was only temporary, and the pair were at loggerheads once more when the enlightened Kate advised young Sandra Murray to go to the family-planning clinic in York. Ferrenby would clearly have to dragged kicking and screaming into the 1960s.

Then there was Blaketon. Kate's hopes that moving to the country would enable her to see more of her husband were proving somewhat optimistic. Blaketon expected him to be permanently on duty and didn't care how it affected his domestic life. When Nick arrived home shattered in the early hours, Kate allowed him to sleep in the following morning, refusing to wake him even when Blaketon phoned demanding to know why he hadn't reported in for work. He and Kate were on a collision course.

But Kate's gripes paled into insignificance compared with the twenty-year-old feud between two rival farmers, Matthew Chapman and Dick Radcliffe. Local youths had been playing a series of pranks on the volatile Chapman, who immediately blamed Radcliffe and cut off access to his home. When Dr Ferrenby was called out to visit Radcliffe's sick wife, he was met by a shotgun-wielding Chapman. Trying to clear the barbed wire

> *'I answer the phone. I take your messages. But I will not be a doormat for that man's ego.'*
>
> *– Kate Rowan puts Nick straight about Oscar Blaketon*

Kate Rowan knew she faced a struggle to drag Aidensfield GP Dr Alex Ferrenby into the 1960s.

Unhinged farmer Matthew Chapman (James Cosmo) took long-standing rival Dick Radcliffe (Paul Copley) prisoner following a series of pranks by local youths.

barring his path, the elderly doctor stumbled and injured his wrist and, unable to drive, was forced to swallow his pride and ask Kate to help out with his practice. As Chapman took Radcliffe prisoner, a siege situation developed, which was finally resolved by Kate's discovery that Mrs Radcliffe and Chapman had once been betrothed. In despair, Chapman now tried to shoot himself but Nick bravely managed to disarm him before he could pull the trigger. Through gritted teeth, Blaketon expressed his gratitude for Kate's assistance. An understanding of sorts had been reached. And Ferrenby asked her if she would consider joining the practice on a permanent basis.

After some thought, Kate bit the bullet and accepted Ferrenby's offer. However, any illusions she had that her husband would ever be off duty were shattered when they were invited to a wedding and he ended up arresting the best man for drug pushing. They didn't receive too many wedding invitations after that!

The tension between husband and wife was heightened by a CND rally at the

---

## Music in Episode One

**'Always Something There To Remind Me'**
– Sandie Shaw

**'Hippy Hippy Shake'**
– The Swinging Blue Jeans

**'Stranger on the Shore'**
– Acker Bilk

**'Boom Boom'**
– The Animals

Fylingdales early-warning station. The guest speaker was a left-wing politician, Paul Melthorn, one of whose aides, Julian Cantley, was arrested by Nick following a fracas at the Aidensfield Arms. Melthorn wasted no time in accusing Nick of police harassment and of hitting Cantley. To make matters worse, Kate admitted to knowing Melthorn from her student days and to believing in disarmament. Nick was beginning to find out a lot about his wife. He strongly advised her against attending the rally, so when he spotted her there – unaware that she was present on official business – he jumped to the wrong conclusion.

*'I don't want to become old, reliable Dr Rowan, ranked one above the nit nurse. I don't want to become part of the scenery.'*
*– Kate growing restless*

Peace was restored to the Rowan household once the truth was revealed, but the quiet rural life that Nick and Kate had dreamed of seemed an awful long way away.

A CND rally at Fylingdales early-warning station created tension between Nick and Kate Rowan who were in danger of finding themselves on opposite sides of the law.

## A murder solved

Nick thought he had probably seen the back of murder cases when he left London, so he was shocked to become involved with one within a

Dr Kate Rowan examining the lifeless body of former detective Andrew Gerrard.

few weeks of his arrival in Aidensfield. What was more, the victim was a retired senior detective with Scotland Yard, ex-Detective Chief Superintendent Andrew Gerrard. His body was found in his home one Sunday morning while his wife Muriel and elderly mother-in-law, Victoria Wainwright, were at church. He had been shot twice. Two detectives came up from London to investigate the killing and pursued the theory that Gerrard had been murdered by an old gangland adversary. One of the pair, DC Jack Langford, was an old friend of Nick's. Kate was horrified to discover that Blaketon had arranged for Langford to stay at the police house – not least because it was her and Nick's special anniversary dinner. For Kate, three was definitely a crowd, especially when Langford later tried it on with her. Langford got no further with his investigation than he did with Kate, since it was Nick who eventually cracked the case.

Acting on information received from Dr Ferrenby, via Kate, Nick learned that Gerrard had been beating his wife for years. Suspicion then fell on Mrs Gerrard, but Nick did a spot of detective work of his own and realised that Mrs Wainwright had the perfect opportunity to commit murder. That morning, she had crept back to the house from church along a back path and had shot her brutal son-in-law under cover of the church bells. When she saw her daughter being arrested for murder, she could keep her secret no longer and blurted out the awful truth to Nick. Not for the first time, the local man had put one over on the boys from the Met.

Nick's success in solving the Gerrard murder resulted in him being headhunted by

Oscar Blaketon had made it his mission in life to bring Greengrass to justice so he was delighted to nail the old rogue for sheep rustling.

Scotland Yard to join an elite drugs team. The job would have meant promotion to sergeant but would also have necessitated moving back to London. Kate was furious and left him in no doubt as to her feelings.

While Nick agonised over whether to go through with the interview, a local lad, Alan Maskell – with whom the Rowans had become friendly – fled to London after skipping bail on a charge of being an accessory to car theft. Nick offered to look for Maskell while he was in London. His search took him to some dubious clubs in the Portobello Road, one of which was suddenly the target of a drugs raid by the police.

Before he knew it, Nick had been arrested with the other suspects on a trumped-up charge of possession. When Nick revealed his identity and filed an official complaint on the grounds that the drugs had been planted by the police,

he was told by his prospective boss at the Yard to forget what he had seen and drop the complaint. The incident reminded Nick precisely why he had wanted to leave the Met in the first place.

Back in Aidensfield, Oscar Blaketon was an unusually happy man. He had finally got a conviction against Greengrass – fined £100 for sheep rustling.

### Did you know?

Derek Fowlds's favourite Heartbeat moment came in Episode One at 3 o'clock in the morning, crawling through the undergrowth with Billy Simons, Mark Jordon and Nick Berry and saying to each other *'This show will never last'*.

## Kate's kidnap ordeal

On her way to a remote farm to treat a sick child, Amy Reddle, Kate spotted the elderly widower Frank Milner slumped by the side of the road. Kate had treated him the previous day and instinctively stopped her car to help. But, as she assisted the stricken man into the car, he suddenly pulled a gun on her and ordered her to drive to the railway station sidings.

Keeping a cool head and trying to remember all the things Nick had told her to do in a crisis, she left her car headlights on as a clue to her whereabouts before being forced up an abandoned tunnel with a gun at her back.

> ### Did you know?
> Nick Berry's wife, Rachel Robertson, featured in an incest storyline in *Heartbeat*. She appeared in the episode 'Wall of Silence' from Series Two as a teenager, Susan Rawlings, who aborted her brother's child.

Above all, she wanted to know why this was happening to her. Milner revealed that Nick had once arrested his granddaughter Claire back in London and that his evidence had helped convict her on a charge of killing her brutal lover. She later hanged herself in prison.

Kate Rowan being kidnapped at gunpoint by disturbed widower Frank Milner (Peter Barkworth). She went on to suffer a terrifying ordeal in a disused railway tunnel.

> ## Celebrity Sightings – **Series One**
> The veteran actress **Jean Anderson** played the murderess Victoria Wainwright; the sixties satirist **Eleanor Bron** appeared as a member of a family of travellers in the episode 'Outsiders'; **Annette Crosbie** played the con woman Penelope Stirling; and, before appearing as Roy Glover in Emmerdale, **Nicky Evans** turned up as a local teenager, Graham Thompson, one of the youths who tormented farmer Chapman.

Now Milner had come to avenge her death.

When Nick discovered that Kate had not arrived at the farm, he became concerned. Fortunately, Greengrass, out poaching, had spotted her abandoned car near the old tunnel. Nick crept into the tunnel, where Kate was trying to appeal to Milner's better nature. She told her captor that she had to get to the farm to give a little girl a lifesaving injection. Sensing that Milner was beginning to waver, she decided to take her chances and stood up ready to leave, only for Milner to turn the gun on himself. Just then, unseen by Milner, Nick arrived, but Kate motioned for him to keep still. Calmly, she persuaded Milner to hand over the gun. With the ordeal over, Kate's first visit was to Amy Reddle.

## Smarter than Alec

One night Nick spotted lights on in the Aidensfield Arms well after closing time and went to investigate. Inside he was taken hostage at gunpoint by three robbers wearing boiler suits and balaclavas, and then dumped in the cellar along with Greengrass and the landlord, George Ward. The raiders left without saying a word, having emptied the contents of the till and relieved Greengrass of a brace of poached

*'We hardly ever see Nick between shots because he's always reading through a huge pile of football magazines.'*
*– Niamh Cusack on working with Nick Berry*

pheasants. The captives were freed in the morning, when a drayman came to deliver beer to the pub, but a few days later there was another armed robbery, this time at the post office.

The only lead had been supplied by a drunken Greengrass, who put forward the name of Alec Robinson, a man with a record for armed robbery but now apparently going straight. Nick and Bellamy interviewed Alec's wife Nell and daughters Susan and Jean, who revealed that Alec had gone off with another woman. However, Dr Ferrenby's medical records showed that a prescription for Alec Robinson had recently been collected by Nell. Under questioning, Nell confessed that Alec had suffered a fatal heart attack during a robbery a short while back and had been dumped on their doorstep by his accomplices. In order to claim National Assistance, the family had concealed his death and buried him at night.

Bellamy and Nick were increasingly suspicious and, on a return visit to the Robinson house, they noticed that Susan and Jean both had expensive new music equipment. Susan tried to make a run for it and, cornered by Bellamy, threatened Nick with a gun. Nell admitted that she had taken up her husband's profession after his death and had masterminded the spate of robberies. Her idea was simply to make enough money to pay off her debts but the girls had insisted on continuing. Frightened that someone was going to get hurt, Nell persuaded Susan to give herself up.

---

**Did you know?**
Bill Maynard first wore Greengrass's old army boots in the 1972 film **Adolf Hitler – My Part In His Downfall** by Spike Miligan and subsequently in the TV series **Oh No – It's Selwyn Froggit** and **The Gaffer**. The boots finally went into retirement when Bill left the series in 2000.

## Foot-and-mouth tragedy

In an eerily prophetic storyline, one of Nick's most heartbreaking duties followed an outbreak of foot-and-mouth disease at Reg Manston's farm. Manston had spent years building up his pedigree herd, only for it to be contaminated by sheep bought by his slovenly neighbour, Sam Carver. When the slaughterman arrived to destroy the herd, Manston tried to keep them at bay with a shotgun until Nick quietly convinced him that there was no alternative. Shots rang out, followed by a huge funeral pyre. At the end of the day's slaughter, Manston wandered off up the moor, accompanied by his faithful sheepdog. When he failed to return by nightfall, his son reported him missing. A search of the moor the following morning discovered Manston's body in an isolated spot, his shotgun and dog by his side. It had all been too much for him to take.

# chapter 2

# A New Face At The Inn

If Aidensfield seemed quiet and staid to Nick and Kate after the bright lights of London, all that changed with the arrival in the village of Gina Ward. The eighteen-year-old niece of George Ward, landlord of the Aidensfield Arms, bubbly Gina moved to Yorkshire from Liverpool, where she had been a persistent offender.

## Dedicated Follower of Fashion

It was a condition of Gina's probation that she go to live in the country with her uncle so that she could be removed from temptation. Fashion-conscious Gina didn't take long to make her mark in her new surroundings, her singing ability winning her a talent contest at her uncle's pub.

George was pleased to have her around. After his trauma at the hands of the Robinson women, he was glad of the company and, besides, a medical complaint which made him tired meant that he needed help to run the pub. His new barmaid was just what the doctor ordered.

## The reluctant bridegroom

Bellamy's girlfriend, Jennifer Galvin, was pregnant, and in sixties Aidensfield that meant only one thing: marriage. Bellamy knew he had no choice, but was not exactly relishing the prospect of his wedding day. His stag night was held at the Aidensfield Arms and at the end an extremely drunk Bellamy was taken outside and handcuffed to a lamppost. But he was then beaten over the head by someone and was later found unconscious by Greengrass.

Jennifer called off the wedding the following day because she had lost the baby. Suddenly Bellamy's

Dedicated follower of fashion Gina Ward came to Aidensfield to escape a troubled past in Liverpool.

reluctance was replaced with an overwhelming desire to go through with the wedding. But when he called round at Jennifer's house, he discovered Jennifer in bed with her previous boyfriend, Peter, whom Bellamy immediately recognised as his assailant outside the pub. At least he had the consolation of arresting him.

## Greengrass strikes it rich

Greengrass came into unexpected wealth when he sold a patch of waste land to the Ministry of Defence at a handsome profit. Revelling in his new-found status, he promptly went out and bought a racehorse and a garish pink Cadillac.

## Did you know?

Chain-smoking, boiled egg-eating Alf Ventress, is played by non-smoking, boiled egg-hating, William Simons. He was alarmed by Alf's idiosyncrasies when he first read the **Heartbeat** scripts, but he has got round the problem by always smoking herbal cigarettes.

## A night to remember

Nick was warned that a violent armed robber, Stevie Walsh, was heading for Aidensfield, having just been released from prison. The proceeds from his most recent crime had never been found but his wife Ellen still lived in the area with her boyfriend Roy. Nick learned from Kate that Mrs Walsh was heavily pregnant and decided to drive out to the Walshes' isolated cottage in a raging blizzard to warn Ellen and Roy that Stevie might be on his way home.

As the snow continued to fall, power to the village was cut off and roads became virtually impassable. It was not exactly a convenient moment for Mrs Walsh to go into labour. Kate managed to borrow a Land Rover and plough her way out to the cottage to help to deliver the baby, but there were complications, so she attempted to drive Ellen and Roy back down to Aidensfield. On the way, the Land Rover skidded and ended up in a ditch.

When Greengrass came into some money after selling a patch of wasteland to the Ministry of Defence, he demonstrated his new-found wealth by driving around in a pink Cadillac...until it was destroyed in a fire.

Gina Ward comforting her injured brother Barry in the wake of the Aidensfield train crash.

As conditions deteriorated, Nick heard that the Aidensfield train had crashed on frozen points just outside the station. Among the passengers were Stevie Walsh, Gina's brother Barry (visiting from Liverpool) and Dr Ferrenby. A train with a snowplough had been summoned but was not expected to arrive for several hours. In the meantime, with the village now completely cut off, Nick had to take command of dealing with the emergency.

The locals turned out in force to ferry the injured to the village hall, where Stevie Walsh (who had done an electrical course in prison) fixed up a generator so at least there was some power. Gina's brother had sustained a broken leg but of more concern was Dr Ferrenby, who was walking about in a daze, seemingly oblivious of what was going on around him.

When Stevie Walsh learned that his wife was in labour, he jumped on a tractor and drove off into the night. He managed to rescue Kate, Ellen and Roy and tow them back to the village hall, where Ellen gave birth to a baby girl. As dawn broke, Stevie headed off again and this time Nick followed him to the cottage, where he was in the act of retrieving the missing loot from his last robbery.

Mindful of the favour Stevie had unwittingly done him by rescuing Kate, Nick agreed to let him go on condition that he hand over the cash.

## Bellamy in trouble

Bellamy's dedication to duty had occasionally left a little to be desired, and so it was when an Ashfordly pawnbroker's was burgled one night at a time that Bellamy should have been patrolling the area. The only clue to the break-in was the sound of a Mini van with a dodgy exhaust roaring away from the shop in a hurry. Acting on an anonymous tip-off, Nick found some of the stolen goods in a lockup rented in

*'I think of Bellamy as a YTS Jack the Lad. Although he joined the force to improve his sex life, he never gets the girl.'*
*– Mark Jordon*

Bellamy's name. Although Nick was certain that his colleague had been stitched up, Bellamy was suspended pending further enquiries..

Trying to unravel the web that was Bellamy's love life, Nick discovered that he had

25

been seeing a local girl by the name of Debbie, who was also the girlfriend of a local gangster, Jack Scarman. Debbie admitted to Nick that she and Bellamy had been together on the night of the break-in. She also revealed that, when she tried to leave him, Scarman had had her beaten up by a thug called Eddie Mooney, and Eddie Mooney just happened to drive a souped-up Mini van.

Nick and Bellamy wasted no time in arresting Mooney and found the rest of the stolen goods at his house. They never were able to prove that Scarman had framed Bellamy, but at least Bellamy was reinstated. He would just have to be more careful about his choice of girlfriends in future. And pigs might fly!

## Ferrenby's farewell

Dr Alex Ferrenby had never been the same since the train crash and having also suffered the trauma of a break-in at the surgery some weeks before, Kate was becoming increasingly worried about his health. But he insisted on going off on a fishing holiday and while away, became disoriented and drowned. The post-mortem revealed that he had been suffering from a slow brain haemorrhage. Villagers turned out in force for his funeral.

Out of the blue, Nick received a phone call from Kate's recently widowed Aunt Eileen to ask whether she could visit them. Nick assumed that Eileen simply fancied a change of scenery and was puzzled when Kate seemed uneasy about the whole affair. On arrival in Aidensfield, Eileen informed them that her late husband, Arthur, had left a sizable legacy to Kate, but, to Nick's amazement, Kate said

> Celebrity Sightings – **Series Two**
> **Peter Barkworth** played Frank Milner, Kate's kidnapper; the former Fine Young Cannibals singer **Roland Gift** played an army deserter, Ken Marston, in 'Over the Hill'; **Dorothy Tutin** guested as a crime writer, Amanda Young, in the episode 'A Talent For Deception'; and **Hugo Speer**, one of the stars of **The Full Monty**, appeared as Chris Rawlings, son of Lord Ashfordly's head keeper.

she couldn't possibly accept it. Nick pointed out that, with her having to move her surgery out of Ferrenby's house, the money was just what they needed, but Kate flatly refused to discuss the matter.

Later, Kate admitted that in her days as a medical student, she had lodged with Eileen and Arthur and one day she had found Uncle Arthur in bed with another woman. He had tried to bribe Kate into keeping quiet and she moved out immediately. Now she felt that the legacy was a continuation of his bribery. But, when Eileen revealed that she knew all about Arthur's womanising and maintained that the money was a gift from both of them, Kate finally accepted it and donated the cash to a charity in memory of Dr Ferrenby.

## Oscar Blaketon's secret

It was only when Nick happened to see Blaketon at a school football match cheering on a lad from Pickering that Ventress disclosed that the boy in question was Blaketon's son,

Graham. Until then, hardly anyone knew that Blaketon even had a son. It certainly wasn't something he talked about, not least because the split from his wife, Joan, had been decidedly acrimonious. Even now Blaketon's preferred method of contact with his ex-wife was through a solicitor; hers was through a medium.

Then one Friday night, Tiny Weedon, the disc jockey at the weekly disco at the village hall, was chased and attacked by three youths, who then rifled his pockets. A witness identified one of the assailants as Graham Blaketon. The news came as a body blow to Sergeant Blaketon who, aware that he would not be able to run the investigation personally, handed it over to officers from Division. When Joan turned up, she immediately accused her ex-husband of being a stickler for the rules and of not having the boy's interests at heart. Nick's enquiries led him to believe that the attackers had stolen drugs from Tiny Weedon. Blaketon immediately rounded on his son and accused

*Above:* Blaketon faced a dilemma when his son Graham landed in trouble with the police.

*Left:* Kate's Aunt Eileen, a kind and thoughtful woman who proved her worth many times during her time in Aidensfield.

him of being involved in drugs, whereupon Graham broke down and confessed to the mugging, but said that they had simply been trying to stop Weedon pushing drugs to youngsters. They had destroyed all the drugs they had seized. Hearing this, Joan asked

Blaketon to have the matter hushed up. After all, Weedon was the real criminal. But Blaketon wouldn't hear of it. Joan angrily told Blaketon that he was still every bit as blinkered as he had been when he destroyed their marriage. However Blaketon managed to use the incident as the first step towards re-establishing a relationship with his son.

## Badger baiting

Nick and Kate were playing darts in the Aidensfield Arms one night when David Stockwell, a mentally retarded man in his thirties, ran into the pub, clearly upset about something. Kate managed to calm him down and glean from him the information that his mother, Florence, had been knocked down by a Land Rover near their isolated cottage in the woods. David said that he had heard dogs barking and had gone to investigate, hotly pursued by his mother, who was telling him to get back into bed.

At the scene of the accident, Nick found a piece of broken headlamp. But, when Nick called on the Stockwells the following day, he heard a different story. Florence was insisting that she had simply fallen over: there was no vehicle involved.

Animal-loving David Stockwell helped trap a gang of callous badger baiters.

### Did you know?

In David Lonsdale's debut episode about badger baiting, the badger they used was a stuffed traffic victim. David had to pull a loop to make his tongue go in and out. They had wanted to use a real one, but, according to badger experts, the risk to David's fingers and nose was too high!

In the meantime, David was out collecting firewood when he stumbled across a badger sett that had been dug out. A dead badger lay nearby with another wounded animal a few yards away. He took the injured badger to Kate, who cleaned it up but said there was nothing more that she could do. So David took it home, kept it warm and fed it.

While investigating the mystery Land Rover, Nick, too, found the broken badger sett and persuaded Greengrass to help him identify further setts. Greengrass confirmed that he had heard the baiters and their terriers out in the woods at the dead of night. Nick tried to pressure David into telling him what really happened, but succeeded only in upsetting him. Overhearing Nick's line of enquiry, Blaketon disclosed that a circular from Division had warned that so-called 'sportsmen' from Middlesbrough were believed to be in the area on the lookout for animals to bait.

Harry Capshaw, a local delivery man specialising in animal feeds, visited Florence in hospital to sort out their financial arrangement. He then leaned on David, promising him the princely sum of ten shillings for each badger sett he identified. David was appalled at the suggestion and went straight to Nick, who decided to set a trap for the baiters. So David told Capshaw that he had found a sett but, when the diggers arrived with their terriers, the police were waiting. A furious fight ensued, which gave Blaketon the satisfaction of knowing that he could additionally charge Capshaw and his men with assaulting police officers. All in all, a good night's work.

## A taxing time for Greengrass

Greengrass was sailing closer to the wind than usual. Punters thought they were onto a bargain when they bought shares in his racehorse Agamemnon (the steed purchased as a result of his Ministry of Defence windfall) – until they discovered that he had sold the horse several times over. He may have managed to wriggle out of that situation but his next adversaries were altogether more formidable – the Inland Revenue. Two tax inspectors called on him and pointed out that he owed capital gains tax on the land deal, not to mention the fact that he hadn't filled in any tax returns for the past fifteen years. Greengrass protested that he hadn't earned anything over that period but the inspectors decided to assess his income from poaching.

Greengrass thought they were bluffing but, when Nick warned him that the bailiffs were on their way,

**Did you know?**

In the original books, Greengrass was described as a 'skinny ferret of a man', while Blaketon was the big, burly one.

Greengrass's lurcher dog Alfred was wrongly accused of being the 'Beast of the Moors'.

Greengrass realised it was time for action. He loaded all his furniture onto a truck, buried a suitcase full of money, and set off with his truck and horse box for the Inland Revenue office in York. There, he deposited his furniture, his horse box and his horse in lieu of the debt.

But Greengrass faced an even greater loss when Alfred was accused of being the 'Beast of the Moors', a fearsome creature that had mutilated dozens of sheep in the area. Unfortunately, Alfred had no alibi for the time of the attacks, because he had been missing from home for several days. When he did finally return, he was covered in white paint. The following day a farmer shot Alfred as the dog ran across fields.

Greengrass was taken to court and the farmer's evidence, coupled with the suspicious paint, persuaded the magistrates to order the wounded Alfred to be destroyed. Before the order could be carried out, a distraught Greengrass managed to smuggle his faithful hound from the police station and, when the true culprit was unmasked, Alfred's reputation was restored. Shortly afterwards, Greengrass was confronted by a woman complaining that Alfred had been mating with her two pedigree bitches despite her throwing a tin of white paint over him. The proud Greengrass immediately demanded a stud fee for his dog.

## Rabies epidemic

In the wake of Dr Ferrenby's death, Kate had some tough decisions to make. A friend asked her to join a new group practice in York but, while Kate was envious of the facilities there, she felt too committed to Aidensfield. Then she received a letter from a Dr James Radcliffe in Whitby, proposing that they set up a joint practice in the area. This seemed far more appealing, and so Kate decided to give it a go.

After initial hostility from Dr Radcliffe's receptionist, Kate settled in nicely and soon had a flu epidemic to deal with. But that was positively trivial compared with what was waiting around the corner. It all started when a local garage mechanic, Jim Swaby, called into Kate's Aidensfield surgery, complaining of headaches. His condition worsened as the day wore on and, when Nick took a new police car to Swaby's garage, he found Swaby experiencing violent spasms. Swaby was rushed to Ashfordly Hospital, where Kate pronounced suspected rabies, a diagnosis confirmed by Dr Radcliffe.

While Nick urgently reported the findings back to Blaketon, the doctors endeavoured to discover from Swaby whether he had been bitten by or come into contact with animals recently. Swaby recalled seeing a left-hand-drive car come into the garage with a dog in the back and thought the occupants were camping in the area. Before he could be of any more help, Swaby died.

A police search was launched of local camp sites and the chief suspects were identified as the Halstead family, who, according to ferry records, had travelled over from Germany in a left-hand-drive Mercedes.

Road blocks were set up in the hope of containing the outbreak and instructions were issued for stray animals to be destroyed and for all domestic pets to be kept indoors. Major Mike Halstead and his wife were soon traced, but there was no sign of their son

Following Alex Ferrenby's death, Kate Rowan set up a joint practice with Whitby-based Dr James Radcliffe.

Jamie, who had apparently gone off to look for the dog. Nick and Greengrass scoured the woods and eventually found Jamie moments after he had

*'You've got a lovely touch. Nice perfume, too. My doctor just smells of carbolic. When I have the stitches out, I'll make sure it's just the two of us, Mrs Rowan.'*
*– Ventress turning on the charm*

been bitten by his dog. As the animal was about to attack again, Greengrass shot it. Major Halstead

With a little help from fishing fanatic Ventress, Nick Rowan went undercover at sea to crack a counterfeit smuggling ring.

was subsequently charged with illegally smuggling an animal into the country.

## Nick undercover

A directive from above led Nick to be sent undercover to Whitby to investigate a counterfeit smuggling ring. His cover was Ventress, who took an annual fishing holiday in Whitby but was not known there as a police officer. While Ventress and Nick went out in a boat, he watched his two fishing friends, Walter and Cedric, setting out to sea. Nick spotted

Cedric pick up a floating container and bring it back to shore and, when the opportunity arose, he sneaked a look inside the container and found it stuffed full of newly minted five-pound notes. Later, Nick saw another man, Hesketh, arrive to collect the container, from which he handed Cedric a bundle of notes.

Acting on orders from Inspector Murchison, who was keen to catch Cedric in possession of the forged notes, Ventress arranged a game of poker with his old friends. Nick won the game and, when he was given the counterfeit money by Cedric, he revealed that he and Ventress were policemen. Cedric was charged with smuggling but struck a deal whereby the police would recommend leniency if he grassed on his bosses. Sure enough, the ship delivering the rest of the containers was tricked into crossing the three-mile limit, whereupon its crew and cargo were seized by police and customs officers. Hesketh

*'When we're out filming on the moors I can't get away with wearing thermals underneath because Gina's clothes are so skimpy there's nowhere to hide them! Luckily most of the time I'm in the warmth of the pub.'*

*– Tricia Penrose*

was arrested when he went to collect the consignment from Cedric.

## Gina's terrifying experience

Following a police rugby match, players and supporters gathered at the Mermaid Inn, Whitby, where Gina flirted with Bellamy and another officer, Gibson. At the end of the evening, Gina drove back towards Aidensfield alone. Along the dark, narrow moorland lanes, she suddenly became aware that she was being followed. As the car behind edged

ever closer, Gina panicked and stalled the engine. With no houses nearby, she instinctively ran into the woods but was soon caught and overpowered by her pursuer. He began to attack her, only to be frightened off by the sound of a shrieking pig. Gina ran home sobbing.

Gina was interviewed by the only female officer to hand – Inspector Murchison – who accused her of being drunk and concocting the story of the attack to cover up the fact that she had had an accident. She overstepped the mark even further when she suggested that Gina had led Bellamy on. Gina insisted that she had simply asked Bellamy to sit in her car until Gibson left the pub because he had been pestering her all evening.

Nick was sent to Whitby to question Gibson, taking with him another Whitby officer, Little, who was also a member of the rugby team. Gibson's family reacted angrily to his being under suspicion and the following day they openly threatened George and Gina. This was the last straw for Gina. Disillusioned by Murchison's lack of sympathy, she announced that she was dropping the charges. Murchison felt that her tough line had been vindicated.

Nick was sure that Gina was telling the truth and concerned that Gibson may have got away with a serious crime, so he asked Little to keep an eye on him. On their next visit to the Whitby pub, Nick and Kate heard that the barmaid, Lizzie, had gone home early because someone had been following her. Nick decided to investigate and intervened just as Lizzie was about to be attacked. The would-be assailant ran off and Nick saw Lizzie safely to her home, not knowing that someone was waiting inside. As Nick headed off, he was alerted by Lizzie's screams and rushed to the rescue. There he discovered the identity of the mystery attacker: Little. Gina subsequently picked out Little at an identity parade but the whole incident had proved so traumatic that she considered leaving Aidensfield and returning to Liverpool. It took all of Nick's and Kate's persuasive powers to get her to stay.

## Troubled times

Nick and Kate were going through one of their sticky patches, invariably caused by one or the other working long hours. So, when Kate found

> 'Heartbeat *is all about the "good old days". They probably never existed, but it's nice to think they did.'*
> – Nick Berry

herself pregnant, her feelings were decidedly mixed. At first she fought shy of telling Nick, and, when she did eventually get round to it, she shocked him by saying that she was contemplating bringing up the child on her own. It hadn't occurred to Nick that things were that bad between them, but before they could discuss it further he realised he was late for work. Same old problem. Later, Nick discussed Kate's pregnancy with Blaketon and admitted that he was thinking of giving up the job. Kate's confidant was Radcliffe, who suggested that they might rearrange their patient list so that Kate could spend more time in Aidensfield.

Both Nick and Kate were then called out to the church, where a man had fallen from the tower onto the roof while in the act of stealing lead. Nick objected strongly when Kate volunteered to climb onto the roof to check out the man's injuries, but she told him that it was her job. He had no option but to let her go ahead. The rescue went smoothly but back at the surgery Kate received a telling-off from Radcliffe, who chastised her for risking her pregnancy and advised her to get her priorities right. When she arrived home, she apologised to Nick for being so thoughtless and for ruining

---

### Celebrity Sightings – **Series Three**

**Dora Bryan** appeared as Jane, a widow bullied into moving out of her cottage by a local property developer; **Julie T. Wallace** played the pig farmer and grave robber Betty Sutch in the episode 'Father's Day'; and **Freddie 'Parrot Face' Davies** played a Whitby arcade owner when the Aidensfield Arms hired a coach to the coast to hear Gina sing.

Although pregnant, Kate Rowan risked life and limb to climb on to the church roof to check the condition of Private Michael Foster who had fallen from the tower while stealing lead.

what should have been their special day.

## A happy reunion

On a visit to an elderly patient, Hannah Stockdale, who lived at Scar Top Farm, Kate was shown a photograph of Hannah's twin sons, both of whom were killed in World War One. But, when Kate asked about the girl in the photo, Hannah immediately clammed up.

Meanwhile, Howard Franklin arrived in Aidensfield, lamenting the fact that he had picked up the wrong suitcase on the train. To complicate matters, his own suitcase contained the ashes of his late wife, Liza, who, it emerged, was Hannah Stockdale's estranged daughter. Howard needed Hannah's permission to bury Liza in the family plot but the old woman, while shocked to hear of her daughter's death, was not prepared to listen to Howard's pleas. When she was called out again to treat Hannah's heart condition, Kate found out more about the long-running feud. It seemed that Hannah blamed Howard for influencing her sons to join up and, by implication, for their subsequent deaths. She also held Howard responsible for the fact that Liza never replied to Hannah's letter. Hannah had not seen her daughter since.

> 'Nick Rowan feels fulfilled as a village bobby. He loves the countryside, the people and the lifestyle. His wife is the quietly ambitious one.'
>
> – Nick Berry

---

### Celebrity Sightings – **Series Four**

**Twiggy** played Lady Janet Whitly in the Christmas episode 'A Winter's Tale', which also featured **Bruce Jones** (as Fred Parkin) before he went on to play Les Battersby in **Coronation Street**; **Thora Hird** and **Frank Finlay** appeared together as Hannah Stockdale and her son-in-law Howard Franklin; **Tim Healy** played the smuggler Cedric Shanks; **Tony Booth** turned up as Greengrass's rival Napper Minto; and **Jenny Agutter** played the duplicitous aristocrat Susannah Temple-Richards in the episode 'Fair Game'.

---

Nick managed to trace the missing suitcase, which had been picked up in error by Hannah's granddaughter, Margaret, who was on her way to Scar Top Farm. When Margaret arrived, Hannah opened the suitcase and found the urn containing Liza's ashes. She was told that Liza had received the letter, but, because Howard had been blamed for the family deaths, Liza's first loyalty had been to him, and so she had never responded. After much deliberation, Hannah finally allowed her daughter to come home, and she was buried in the family plot.

## Christmas cheer

When eight-year-old Danny Parkin, suffering from TB, came out of hospital to visit his family for Christmas, his father Fred dreamed aloud of being able to send him to a Swiss sanatorium. There was little likelihood of that, since Fred had recently been made redundant; but two of Danny's siblings, Ellie and Ronnie, overheard the wish and decided to do something about it. Unfortunately, the fundraising method they chose was to sell Christmas trees – after first stealing them from the estate of the local landowner, Lady Janet Whitly. Furthermore, they 'borrowed' Greengrass's truck as their means of transporting the trees. Greengrass naturally came under suspicion, until Fred found the truck parked at the end of his garden and Ellie and Ronnie hiding Christmas trees in the shed. Given the motive, Nick asked Lady Whitly not to press charges, but she remained defiant until she received a visit from Ellie, who offered a five-pound note by way of compensation. Thinking back to her own impoverished childhood in the East End of London, Lady Whitly had a sudden change of heart. Not only did she drop the charges but she also agreed to pay for Danny's treatment in Switzerland. As the Parkin family rejoiced at the village concert, Kate suddenly groaned and clutched her stomach. The baby was making its presence felt.

### Did you know?

Mark Jordon was once mistaken for a real policeman when he went straight from the set to an off-licence to buy some wine whilst still in costume. He was harangued by the shop-keeper for the late arrival of the police at a local incident. Thinking the woman was joking, he told her that the police couldn't attend sooner because they had been playing a football match. He heard later that she'd made a complaint!

*'Then find something, lad. Bald tyres, bad brakes, bad breath, anything. Just get rid of 'em.'*
*– Blaketon, ordering Nick to move on a family of seemingly law-abiding travellers*

Nick tried to persuade Lady Janet Whitly (Twiggy) to bring Christmas cheer to the impoverished Parkin family.

# chapter 3

# Kate's Tragic Death

It was ironic that when Maggie Bolton, the new district nurse, arrived in Aidensfield, one of her first patients was Dr Kate Rowan, but with Kate hiding her symptoms, her death was a devastating and unforeseen blow.

# The Crying Game

Kate had been suffering from anaemia from the early stages of her pregnancy, but had promised to treat it herself. Maggie gave her iron injections but she was sufficiently concerned about how pale Kate looked to advise her to take another blood test at 36 weeks. Kate chose to send the test off to the hospital under another name and when she rang up for the 'patient's' results she was devastated by what she heard. Nevertheless, she decided to keep the news to herself, apart from discussing the results with a consultant, Mr Faber, still on the pretext that they were those of a patient rather than her own. The consultant advised her that treatment was urgent.

Shortly afterwards, Kate went into labour. Nick, who had been out with Blaketon buying a pram, arrived just as she went into the delivery room. She gave birth to a baby girl, whom they named Sarah.

But Nick's joy at fatherhood was to be short-lived. Maggie discovered that Kate had concealed her serious illness by putting her blood test under a false name. Kate promised that now that the baby had been born safely she would tell Nick. And so, when he next came to visit his wife and daughter, Kate told him the awful truth: that she had acute leukaemia. He vowed that they would fight it together.

Kate returned home with baby Sarah but made Nick swear to keep her illness a secret from their friends in the village. They took their last picnic together as a family up on the moors, but Kate was too tired to stay long. Nick was reluctant to leave his wife for work – all the more so when a haematologist stated that she had

*Above:* Nick and Kate's happiness with their baby was to be tragically short-lived.

*Below:* New district nurse Maggie Bolton discovered that Kate had deliberately hidden the seriousness of her illness.

contracted pneumonia – and was severely reprimanded by Blaketon for his failure to respond to reports of petrol thefts in the area. Overhearing Blaketon's outburst, Kate decided that it was time for Nick to tell his colleagues the truth. Blaketon was mortified to recall the lecture he had given Nick in his ignorance and immediately granted him compassionate leave.

Kate's condition deteriorated alarmingly but she refused to go back to hospital. She knew she was dying and gave Nick instructions about looking after Sarah. Shortly afterwards she died peacefully in her sleep.

There was a full turnout for the funeral, including Kate's Aunt Eileen and Nick's mum, Ruby. Nick's uncharacteristically aggressive behaviour was giving his colleagues cause for concern and, on leaving the churchyard, Ventress had to prevent him beating up the petrol thief.

> *'So this is what you're up to it, is it, Rowan? Playing mummies and daddies. While drawing full pay from the North Riding Constabulary. And while I, Rowan, receive complaints. Complaints about the inefficiency of the village constable. About rudeness, about incompetence. And these complaints come to me because for some unknown reason nobody can contact you.'*
>
> *– Blaketon, berating Nick, unaware that Kate was gravely ill*

Ventress persuaded Nick to attend the wake at the Aidensfield Arms but Nick still blamed the doctors for failing to treat Kate in time. It was only when Maggie pointed out that Kate had deliberately kept her symptoms hidden that he began to see sense. Blaketon took Nick back home but, when Maggie and Eileen arrived not long after, there was no sign of Nick or the baby. Instead they had returned to the waterfall where he and Kate had spent their last day out. In memory of his wife, Nick decided to call the baby Katie.

## Coming to terms

Trying to bring up a baby, keep law and order in Aidensfield and adjust to life without Kate proved a headache for Nick, especially when his regular babysitter went sick. Too proud to accept help from Maggie, Nick had no choice

Nick's colleagues turned out in force for the sombre occasion of Kate's funeral.

*Above:* Ruby Rowan stayed on to mix moral support for son Nick with immoral thoughts towards Oscar Blaketon.

*Right:* To help come to terms with his loss, Nick decided to call the baby Katie in honour of his late wife.

Celebrity Sightings – **Series Five**
**Patricia Hayes** played Flo, a spirited old travelling lady in the episode 'Expectations'; **Mark Addy** from **The Full Monty** played Greengrass's nephew Norma, an expert darts player; **David Neilson** (**Coronation Street**'s Roy Cropper) guested as the schoolteacher Barry Jackson in the episode 'Sophie's Choice'; **The Royle Family**'s **Ralf Little** appeared as Eddie Tinniswood, son of the local burglar Terry Tinniswood; **Una Stubbs** played Anthea Cowley, long-suffering wife of the pompous Special Constable Hector Cowley; and **Kelvin Fletcher** appeared as the schoolboy Colin Ellis before moving to **Emmerdale** as Andy Sugden.

but to smuggle Katie into work, where Bellamy and Ventress attempted to perfect the art of nappy changing in a police cell while avoiding the eagle eye of Blaketon. However, when Maggie inadvertently spilled the beans, Blaketon told Nick he would have to make proper arrangements for the welfare of his daughter. Nick's domineering mum, Ruby, came up from London to stay for a while and tried to persuade him to return to the capital, where she would be able to help more, but Nick was keen to stay in Aidensfield. The man-hungry Ruby set her sights on Blaketon but, before Nick could get too alarmed at the prospect of having his sergeant as his stepfather, Ruby tired of Blaketon's singular lack of romance. And, when Aunt Eileen announced that she was coming to stay, Ruby realised that Aidensfield wasn't big enough for big enough for both of them and headed back

Three men and a baby: Ventress, Bellamy and Blaketon tackle feeding time at the station for baby Katie Rowan. But Blaketon made sure that the arrangement was purely temporary.

to London. Blaketon could count it as a lucky escape.

## Ventress's close encounter

Answering a call to a burglary at the height of a violent storm that had cut all power to Aidensfield, Ventress was dazzled by a powerful light while in the act of parking his car and ended up banging his head on the windscreen. When Nick returned to the car, he found his colleague behaving in an even stranger way than usual. Ventress told him he had been blinded by a bright light near the golf course. They went to investigate, but all they could find was a patch of dry ground amid the puddles.

However, when Maggie examined Ventress for possible concussion, she was puzzled to see that one side of his face appeared to be sunburned. Two independent witnesses – one of them Greengrass – stated that a UFO had landed on the golf course during the storm. That was good enough for Ventress, who decided to file an official report about his close encounter. Blaketon was sceptical about Ventress's story, but Nick thought there was

> ### Did you know?
> Derek Fowlds's favourite singer is Neil Diamond and the cast have regular Neil Diamond theme parties – usually singing until dawn! The cast and crew have even adopted the song 'Sweet Caroline' as the **Heartbeat** anthem.

some truth in it; and, when Maggie arranged for Ventress to be put into a trance by a hypnotist, he relived the episode down to the last detail.

Ventress was put on indefinite sick leave and sent to a psychiatrist, who encouraged him to admit to a temporary mental breakdown in order to avoid embarrassing the authorities. Now more convinced than ever that Alf was not imagining things, Nick began to suspect an official police cover-up over the UFO. He insisted that Ventress stick to his guns and prevented Divisional HQ from discrediting Ventress's mental state by threatening to tell the press the whole story.

## Bero Man strikes again

Aidensfield was in the grip of a series of burglaries carried out by a masked raider nicknamed 'Bero Man' on account of the Bero flour bag worn over his head. Gina was confronted by the intruder one night in her bedroom at the Aidensfield Arms until George chased him away, and soon the entire village was living in fear. Maggie was no exception, particularly when her calls took her to isolated locations such as the sombre Flax farm, where she had to give the miserly Mr Flax his tetanus injection. While there, she witnessed a fierce row between Flax and his awkward teenage daughter Marion, which ended with Marion storming off.

As Maggie made her way back to her car, she was alarmed to see Bero Man running towards her. Fortunately, Maggie managed to drive off in the nick of time. Before long, Nick was investigating another burglary – this time at the Flax house. Marion told Nick that, when Bero Man appeared, she screamed and he ran

Ventress's mental state was called into question after he claimed to have been dazzled by the bright lights of a UFO landing on the local golf course at the height of a storm.

off. There were no other witnesses. A couple of hours later the mysterious Bero Man was seen dancing on a distant burial mound.

Bero Man's next target was Greengrass's place, and after evading capture there he broke into Maggie's house. When Maggie returned home, there was a struggle, leaving Maggie dazed and winded, and once again the masked burglar escaped. Searching Greengrass's house for clues, Nick spotted on the kitchen wall a clock stolen from the Flax home during one of the Bero Man raids. Greengrass said that he bought it from Marion, along with other items. Nick set off for the Flax farm to question Marion and found Maggie cornered by Bero Man. The burglar escaped, only to find his exit blocked by Mr Flax wielding a shotgun. Bero Man had little alternative but to unmask himself. It was Marion Flax, sobbing that she wanted a life and wanted Maggie to be her friend, adding that she might as well be in a real prison as spend the rest of her life at the Flax farm. Maggie didn't know whether to feel sad or relieved.

## An old flame

There was a surprise visitor at the party following baby Katie's christening — Nick's first girlfriend, Jill Criddle, now a sergeant in the Metropolitan Police. Nick was delighted to see her again, although their friendship caused instant gossip in the village. Maggie was particularly curious. Nick soon turned Jill's visit into a busman's holiday when Newcastle CID gave him the task of going undercover to investigate the activities of a Tyneside gangster, Frank Armstrong, who was opening a gambling club in Scarborough.

*'Maggie's quite tough and self-reliant because being a rural nurse she has to jump in that Land Rover and drive off alone across the moors. But she's also totally trustworthy with a good sense of irony. She's my idea of the ideal nurse.'*
*– Kazia Pelka*

Nick suggested that Jill come along for the ride. They spent the evening together at the casino, where Armstrong took a shine to Jill, enabling her to distract him while Nick sneaked into the main office in search of incriminating evidence. He uncovered a map, on which several locations were marked. They turned out to be the sites of racing stables. Nick suspected that Armstrong was out to fix the big race at Ripon the next day and so Bellamy and Ventress were put on overnight guard at the stables of the favourite, Fab Four. They had nothing to report but equine flatulence.

Meanwhile, a horse doper, Billy Black, was in deep with Armstrong over his gambling debts and sought refuge from the gangster's heavies with his old pal Greengrass. When Armstrong's men caught up with him, they ordered him to slow down the favourite in the big race.

Nick and Jill continued to work undercover at the races until Armstrong was tipped off by Billy that they were police officers. Armstrong tricked Jill into leaving with him and then imprisoned her in a horse box. Frantic with worry, Nick pressured Greengrass into revealing which horse Billy was targeting and caught Billy in the act of doping Fab Four. Billy told Nick where to find Armstrong and Jill was rescued unharmed. The next day she left Aidensfield to return to work in London. Nick promised to visit her soon.

## Teflon Terry

If there was one person Blaketon was almost as keen to nail as Greengrass it was the local burglar Terry Tinniswood, known to the police as 'Teflon Terry' because they could never get anything to stick to him. Terry had only recently been released from prison after being framed by Nick's predecessor for a crime he didn't commit. Some called it poetic justice, but now Terry was back to his old ways, breaking into the Wakefields' house. Arthur Wakefield confronted Terry but suffered a fatal heart attack before he could grab him. Arthur's wife, Miriam, saw a man running from the scene – she later picked out Terry from police mug shots – and his holdall was found at the house, although it was clean of fingerprints. Terry was arrested but this time his wife, Rosie, had hired a wily solicitor, Sugden, who made sure his client had a cast-iron alibi. Knowing that he needed solid evidence to prevent a repetition of the last Tinniswood case, Blaketon had no choice but to let him go.

Miriam Wakefield was appalled to learn of Terry's release and conducted a silent campaign against him. She started stalking Terry and Rosie, who reacted angrily and made an official complaint. Miriam protested that she wasn't breaking the law. Terry was beginning to crack under the strain of Miriam's constant surveillance and, when he went missing, a worried Rosie alerted Nick.

Terry was traced to the village show, where he was drunkenly pointing a shotgun at Miriam and threatening to shoot her for making his life a misery. He was arrested and then released, pending a court appearance, but became even more depressed when his wife left him, taking the children with her. Soon afterwards, he turned up at Miriam's house, having slit his wrists. By the time Nick arrived, Miriam had already called an ambulance and started to bandage Terry's wrists. She told Nick that it was justice she was seeking, not vengeance.

### Did you know?

When Derek Fowlds, a Londoner, first read the script, he thought the producers wanted him to play Nick Rowan, because he was the only southern character in it. 'I told my agent I was a bit too old to play Nick and, even when I discovered that they wanted me to play Blaketon, I nearly talked myself out of the job because I wasn't sure I was right for the part.'

assistant. After digging for a while, the JCB hit an obstruction and Greengrass climbed down into the pit to investigate. David tried to move the digger but the bucket fell into the pit, trapping Greengrass. To his horror, Greengrass realised that he was face to face with an unexploded wartime bomb.

David flagged down Nick, who was passing by on his bike. Nick in turn radioed Bellamy to contact the bomb squad and start evacuating the area. The three-man bomb squad arrived,

*Left:* Greengrass landed in an awkward predicament when his excavations unearthed a wartime bomb.

*Below:* Greengrass was freed before the explosion which killed one of the bomb disposal team.

## Greengrass and the unexploded bomb

Ventress had acquired a plot of land for a bungalow and had made the mistake of allowing Greengrass to dig a cesspit. To Ventress's dismay, Greengrass turned up with a rusty old JCB and David Stockwell as his

along with the fire brigade, and a mud-covered Greengrass was winched off the bomb before being taken to a nearby convent for a bath. The local paper reported that two nuns had to be treated for shock.

While Sapper Smith led the delicate task of defusing the bomb, which had started to tick, the police had other worries. A schoolboy railway enthusiast, Colin Ellis, had gone missing, but, when Nick and the boy's mother searched the evacuated home of stationmaster Hutton in search of Colin, they found instead a man's body in one of the bedrooms. Hutton, too, was discovered upstairs. Both Hutton and his wife Sandra denied knowing the dead man. However, when word reached Nick that Sandra Hutton had a lover, everything pointed to a crime of passion.

Nick continued to search for Colin and eventually found him in Hutton's locked shed, accompanied by a collection of stolen railway property. Just then, the bomb exploded, killing Sapper Smith, wrecking Hutton's house and shed and leaving a huge crater behind. A dazed Bellamy remembered seeing Nick in Hutton's garden moments before the explosion. Everyone dug frantically in the rubble and Nick and Colin were rescued unharmed.

Meanwhile, there was the matter of the corpse in what was, until a few minutes ago, Hutton's house. Blaketon was about to charge Hutton with murder when Sandra confessed that her lover had died from a heart attack. All things considered, Blaketon felt that Hutton had already lost enough for one day and decided not to charge him with stealing railway property.

## St Columba's treasure

Climbing a ladder in his library one day, an elderly archaeologist, Professor Brigstocke, toppled and fell, sustaining fatal injuries. His

*'This Shaw Taylor stuff's all very well, but I want results. Division are threatening a permanent CID presence here until this chap's caught. And we don't want that, do we, Ventress?'*

*– Blaketon on the trail of a serial burglar*

body was found the next day by his personal assistant, Mary Secker, who stole a series of documents before calling the police anonymously. When news of the professor's death became public, rumours of buried

Greengrass and Blaketon endured an uncomfortable time trapped in an underground tunnel.

treasure began to circulate in the village – finds from excavations that he had apparently never declared.

Meanwhile, Blaketon had weightier things on his mind – the theft of Lord Ashfordly's trout. Nick and Bellamy were assigned to patrol the river at night, only to be called away to investigate a break-in at Brigstocke's house. There was no sign that anything had been taken but in the officers' absence Greengrass and his undertaker accomplice 'Erbert helped themselves to some more of Lord Ashfordly's trout. His Lordship left Blaketon in no doubt as to the extent of his displeasure.

Greengrass was the obvious suspect but a search of his house revealed nothing. That evening Aunt Eileen cooked Nick a lovely fresh trout – a present from Greengrass. While Nick was looking into a succession of petty thefts with the same modus operandi, Greengrass was hot on the trail of the buried treasure, believed to be hidden in the ruins of St Columba's Abbey. Nick realised that the Brigstocke break-in was one of a series carried out shortly after the occupant had died. 'Erbert worked as a layer-out for all the local undertakers and, when Nick visited his house, he found stolen property. A further call at the undertakers' cold

## Did you know?

During the filming of Kate's last episode, the cast felt as if there was a real death occurring, and as the episode went by, the atmosphere got gloomier and gloomier because they knew Niamh was going.

**Did you know?**

When Nick Berry met Thora Hird, she was very complimentary about his work and the show and they had a long chat. It was only later that Thora admitted that she had mistaken him for the director, and hadn't actually heard a word he'd said to her because, by his own admission, Nick is a bit of a mumbler!

stores revealed Lord Ashfordly's trout.

Oblivious of all this, Blaketon was following Greengrass's every move. Seeing Greengrass's truck covered with a tarpaulin, he climbed in the back to investigate – moments before Greengrass drove off with Blaketon still hiding in the back. The journey took them to the ruins of St Columba's Abbey, where Greengrass entered a tunnel, closely pursued by Blaketon. In his clumsiness, Greengrass caused a rock fall, which blocked the entrance to the tunnel. As Blaketon made his presence known, the two men argued bitterly about what to do next. They decided to head further into the tunnel, but, while they were trying to find another exit, the floor suddenly gave way beneath their feet. Blaketon was injured in the fall, but Greengrass was excited by finding some tin chests. He was convinced that it was the buried treasure until he opened the chests and found just a collection of old Latin manuscripts. A few hours later, with Blaketon feeling the cold, Greengrass decided to burn the documents to keep the pair of them warm.

Help was on its way. Aunt Eileen, who had developed a friendship with Blaketon to the extent of their enjoying a round of golf together, became concerned when he failed to show up for supper and it became apparent that Greengrass was also missing. Nick and Maggie located Greengrass's truck but, with the tunnel entrance blocked, they had to seek an alternative ingress. Eileen told Nick that Mary Secker had borrowed the abbey plans the other day. Mary revealed that she used to work with Brigstocke and realised from the documents she had taken from his house that he had unearthed the abbey library. A secret tunnel was found linking Brigstocke's house to the ruins, and Greengrass and Blaketon were rescued, but Mary was horrified to learn that Greengrass had unwittingly burned the precious historical documents she had been seeking. These documents were the priceless contents of the secret abbey library, and Greengrass had set fire to the St Columba's treasure..

And, if Blaketon thought his ordeal was over, he was wrong. For he and Greengrass ended up in hospital – in adjacent beds.

*'I based him on my drill instructor, because I was in the RAF for national service. I just cut my hair shorter, slicked it back and shouted a lot and Oscar was born.'*

*– Derek Fowlds on Blaketon*

# chapter 4

# Nick And The Schoolteacher

Despite his grief at Kate's death, Nick was slowly adjusting to his life as

a single father, but he never thought he would find new

romance so quickly. The arrival of a very pretty young

schoolteacher in town made him realise

that a solitary life was not

the life for him.

## Little Children

Nick first met primary schoolteacher Jo Weston in the middle of a health scare. He had gone to the school to make enquiries about a man called Carter and his young son, Simon. Despite the fact that Simon was ill, Carter seemed reluctant to take him to a doctor.

It later emerged that Carter had kidnapped the boy from his ex-wife who had hired a private investigator to find him. Meanwhile, Simon's condition was worsening and Gina gave them a lift to the hospital. To Carter's dismay his ex-wife Michelle caught up with him at the hospital. They had a huge row and Carter ran

off. As it became clear that Simon had polio a mass vaccination was organised at the school, but the main concern was the whereabouts of Charles Carter, who was in serious danger of contracting the disease.

Nick launched an urgent search for him, and having remembered seeing him with some fishing tackle decided to check the river in the woods.

He was not the only one in the woods at that time… Jo was on a nature ramble with some schoolchildren and it was she who found Carter collapsed on the ground. And they bumped into each other again at the hospital where Jo offered her condolences for Kate's death. Nick was smitten…

## Greengrass's new job

Luckily for them, Jo and Nick were destined to be thrown together and before he knew it, Nick had been invited by Jo to give a talk to the schoolchildren on road safety.

Greengrass was also busy at the school in his new job as lollipop man. But it wasn't long before he fell foul of motorist Walter Pettigrew, whom he accused of speeding. Pettigrew took umbrage and complained about Greengrass's

Once he'd met Jo, Nick finally started putting his grief behind him.

attitude, although Jo supported the claim that he was driving too fast.

Things got worse for Greengrass when headmistress Mrs Watkins reported a rash of petty pilfering, Greengrass's name was put in the frame and despite protesting his innocence, he was sacked. For once wrongly accused, Greengrass was left licking his wounds until Jo caught two boys stealing from the classroom. He was immediately reinstated as school lollipop man.

The following week Nick and Jo met again when Lord Gillies, Lord Ashfordly's estate manager, complained to Blaketon after the local hunt had been interrupted by a school nature ramble trespassing on private land. Nick was dispatched to the school to talk to Jo about the incident and took the opportunity to ask her out. Three times they met up but on each occasion their date was interrupted when Nick was called out to deal with a case. Jo soon realised that a policeman's lot was not always a happy one.

Life was no sweeter at the Aidensfield Arms, where George and Gina were shocked to learn that Lord Ashfordly, having fallen on hard times, was doubling the rent for the pub. So they introduced bar meals in an attempt to boost their profits. The decision provided an unexpected bonus for Gina, who returned from Liverpool with a new boyfriend in tow, Anton, and persuaded Uncle George to hire him as chef. However, when their passion in the kitchen became a little too heated, so did the cooker, as a neglected chip pan caught fire. Anton had to be treated for serious burns and Eileen had to take his place in the kitchen. Gina's love life seemed doomed to fail.

## Which doctor?

Life was peaceful for shopkeeper Alan Davies until Adrian Shaw moved in next door. Suddenly Davies started receiving a series of threats. It started with nuisance phone calls but escalated into something more sinister when flowers were left on the doorstep of his cottage.

My boy lollipop: Greengrass in a rare attempt at making an honest living.

A stranger called Fenwick was also giving him a hard time. He accosted him and began asking him questions, but Davies insisted that he wasn't the man he was looking for.

Then, one night, Davies was disturbed by an intruder and fled to the police house in his pyjamas. Nick accompanied him back to the cottage, where they found that a photograph of a little girl had been left. Davies did not recognise the child and was even more alarmed when a similar photograph was delivered to his shop.

Davies had no idea who was behind the campaign of intimidation. Blaketon discovered that Davies had once had an affair with the wife of his business partner, Derek Bracewell, and suspected that Davies was fabricating the incidents in order to draw attention to himself. For his part, Bracewell firmly denied any involvement. It was clear that matters were getting out of hand, however, when Davies received a death threat in the form of a mutilated picture of Dr Kildare pinned to his bedroom wall.

Police protection was supplied by Bellamy, who stayed with him in the cottage that night and, on leaving the following morning, told Davies to follow him to Ashfordly police station. As Bellamy drove off, Fenwick and an accomplice broke into the cottage, abducted Davies and took him to a moorland bothy. Shortly afterwards Terry Hunt arrived at the bothy armed with a gun and told Fenwick that he'd got the wrong man. Hunt wanted Dr Graham, the man responsible for killing his daughter when performing an operation while drunk.

Alerted by Greengrass, who had been keeping watch on the bothy, the police arrived and managed to disarm Hunt and free Davies.

> *'The day Ventress joined the police he was looking forward to retirement.'*
> *– William Simons*

Hearing Hunt's story and remembering the expert way in which Adrian Shaw had treated Anton the chef's burns at the Aidensfield Arms, Nick realised that it was Shaw who was really Dr Graham. Nick went to confront him, but arrived too late. The man calling himself Shaw had committed suicide.

## Maggie's hit-and-run nightmare

Susan Watkins worked as housekeeper for the terminally ill Michael Harvey and his son Ronnie. After she took Michael a birthday cake, he stunned her by proposing to her – an announcement that came as an equal shock to Ronnie, who clearly had designs on Susan himself. When Ronnie conveyed his anger, Susan ran away in distress and was later found lying in the road with a head injury, having been knocked from her bicycle by a car. It was Maggie who found her and rang Nick, but, on arriving at the scene, he couldn't help but notice that her car was damaged.

Although Maggie protested her innocence, claiming she herself had been forced off the road by another car, Nick felt obliged to take a paint sample.

In searching for Susan's missing bicycle, Nick took a look at two cars in the Harveys' garage, both of which were in pristine condition. Blaketon was now more convinced than ever that Maggie was the hit-and-run driver. But Nick refused to believe Maggie capable of such a crime and, just as Susan's mother discovered love letters to her daughter from Ronnie, Nick learned that Michael Harvey owned a third car – a Riley.

After forensic tests finally put Maggie in the clear, Nick interrogated Ronnie about his relationship with Susan. He admitted that Susan was his girlfriend but refused to divulge the whereabouts of the Riley, insisting that his father had sold it. With the net closing in, Michael went to the police station, confessed to the hit-and-run and told the police where to find the Riley. However, Nick was sure that Ronnie was involved somehow and told him about his father's confession. Ronnie said that he had hidden the car and the bicycle to protect his father and cover up the accident Nick was still not convinced. Nick was puzzled why Ronnie had not tried to help Susan. Eventually, Ronnie broke down and admitted that it was he who had knocked Susan off her bike accidentally. Thinking he had killed her, he had then fled the scene in a panic.

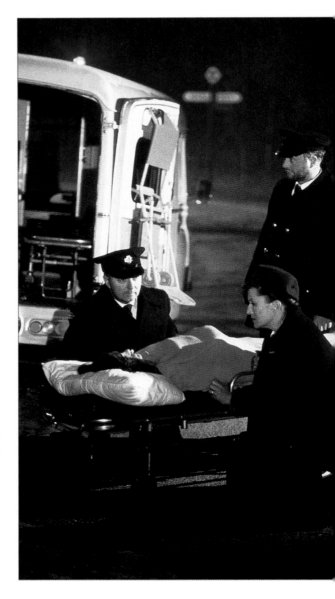

Maggie Bolton comforts hit-and-run victim Susan Watkins – an incident for which Maggie herself was prime suspect.

## The cancelled weekend

Life was very busy for Nick. With a full time job, a baby and his sergeant's exams coming up, Nick had eagerly accepted Jo's offer of a weekend away. However, he hadn't quite got round to breaking the news to Aunt Eileen and, when Jo got in first, Eileen felt hurt that Nick had not mentioned anything to her. Jo, too, was worried. Was Nick ashamed of going away with her so soon after Kate's death? Was he ready for a proper relationship?

Before any of these questions could be answered, Nick was called out to investigate a fire at Ralph Webster's hotel. Webster suspected one of his employees, Brian Rogers, of being responsible for the fire and other acts of sabotage, but Nick traced the accident to an electrical fault and thought Rogers was nothing more than accident-prone. Webster was adamant, however, and, when a guest was injured after falling down a flight of stairs, Webster blamed Rogers for not fixing the stair carpet properly and sacked him on the spot.

The hotel was also being used for a fashion shoot. The photographer, Jansson, called in at the Aidensfield Arms and recruited Gina, Greengrass and Alfred as models to accompany his regular girls, Michelle and Sylvie. Greengrass envisaged the start of a whole new career or, at the very least, a small fee.

Following his dismissal, Brian Rogers went on a drunken binge in Whitby and refused to pay his taxi fare home, threatening the driver with a bottle. The driver told the police, and Nick, who was supposed to be going away with Jo when his shift finished, was sent to reason with Rogers. Nick's words fell on stony ground. Rogers locked himself in his house before reappearing at the door with a gun, forcing Nick to send for backup in the form of Blaketon, Ventress and Bellamy. Acting on Greengrass's advice, they fetched Rogers's formidable mother, Avis, from her workplace. Avis wasted no time in telling her son exactly what she thought of him and persuaded him to let her into the house, but he then took her hostage and dragged her out of sight from the police. A gunshot rang out from within the house.

Meanwhile Jansson was pressing ahead with the shoot at Webster's Hotel, after which Webster kindly drove Michelle and Sylvie back to Aidensfield, leaving Jansson behind to load up the van. Jansson then organised a group photo in the pub but, making an excuse to pop outside, he drove off at speed with Michelle and Sylvie. George discovered that Jansson had stolen cash from the pub and, up at the hotel, a quantity of silver and antiques were missing. Nick was switched from the siege to intercept Jansson and managed to block his getaway.

Back at the Rogers house, Blaketon was about to end the stand-off when Avis opened the front door and announced that her son had fallen asleep. Rogers was taken into custody but refused to be interviewed by anyone but Nick, who therefore had to tell Jo that their weekend away would have to be postponed. Jo was unimpressed to say the least and promptly ended their relationship.

A fashion photographer used his two models as decoys in a series of burglaries.

his injuries. He had been having an affair with the coach driver's wife and the driver had glimpsed them in his rear-view mirror a split second before the crash. The implication was that he had taken his eyes off the road for a fatal moment.

## Alfred and the Masked Marvel

Greengrass was helping a promoter, Pat Starr, to advertise his forthcoming wrestling show in Aidensfield, not only by putting up posters around the village but also by providing board and lodgings for the show's number-one attraction, the Masked Marvel. Alas, Alfred took a bite out of the Marvel, putting the wrestler out of action for a week. As a last-minute replacement, Greengrass recruited a local man, Ken Fairbother, who had been the first to put his name down to fight the Marvel. Ken would be the new Masked Marvel. The first show, with Gina singing as a warm-up act, went down a storm. Ken was such a success as the bogus

---

> Celebrity Sightings – **Series Six**
>
> **Kenneth Cranham** played the rogue haulier Charlie Wallace; **Keeley Hawes** appeared as the photographer's model Michelle in the episode 'Snapped'; **Roger Lloyd Pack** (Trigger from **Only Fools and Horses**) played Reggie Rawlins, an old associate of Greengrass; **Pat Roach** (Bomber from **Auf Wiedersehen, Pet**) appeared as the wrestler, the Masked Marvel; and **Owen Aaronovitch** appeared as the wronged Clive Kenway in the episode 'Obsessions' before making Deirdre's life a misery in **Coronation Street** as the fake airline pilot Jon Lindsay.

---

Jo's attitude remained colder than a North Yorkshire winter until Nick's mother, Ruby, up from London on a surprise visit, had a quiet word with her, as a result of which Jo agreed to give Nick another chance. A condition of the reunion appeared to be dinner with Jo's very middle-class parents, Fiona and Graham.

It was an awkward occasion, made worse by the fact that Jo had neglected to tell her parents that Nick was a widower with a daughter. Mother, in particular, did not approve.

The evening was not improved when news of a coach crash came in. He and Jo dashed from the dinner party in the belief that Eileen and Katie were on the crashed coach. Luckily, they had accepted a lift in a car instead. Bellamy was on the coach, however, with his new girlfriend Marlene, but they escaped unscathed. Less fortunate was Jack Abbott, who died from

*'I used to play golf with a bloke who was a builder and, whenever he used to cheat a bit, he would always screw up his eyes and twitch. It was a dead giveaway. So I gave Greengrass a twitch so that the audience would know when he was telling lies.'*

*– Bill Maynard*

The principals in a wrestling scam. (left to right) The real 'Masked Marvel' (Pat Roach), promoter Pat Starr (Bobby Knutt), impostor Ken Fairbrother (Adam Fogerty) and the ubiquitous Greengrass.

Marvel that Starr decided that he had no further need for the genuine article and fired him. But the indignant Marvel had the last word, threatening to unmask Ken as an impostor in front of the audience unless Starr gave him his job back. Starr may not have had a conscience to wrestle with, but he was worried that he wouldn't have a big name, either. So the real Masked Marvel was reinstated.

## Love-triangle death

After Sylvia Phillips left her husband and family to live with Mike Scott, proprietor of the Black Lion in Ashfordly, her twenty-year-old son Tony vented his anger by hurling a bottle through one of the pub windows. Nick caught Tony in the act but Scott did not want to press charges. Later, Sylvia returned home to talk to her husband Jim, her daughter Vicki and Tony, but a ferocious row developed and a neighbour, Anne Fowles, called out Nick to restore order. Later, Sylvia told Scott that she needed time to think things over. But before she had time to do much thinking, her body was found in a roadside ditch.

It soon became clear that this was not an ordinary hit-and run incident and Detective Sergeant Adams from CID arrived to take charge of the murder investigation. Scott told the police that Sylvia had gone out the previous evening to visit her family, but Jim Phillips denied that she had ever gone to the house. However, a neighbour reported having seen Sylvia enter the house on the night of her death and having heard a violent argument. Confronted with this information, Jim confessed to killing his wife claiming she had fallen and hit her head and, in his panic, he had dumped her body by the roadside. As far as Adams was concerned, it was an open-and-shut case. But nothing in Aidensfield is quite as simple as it first appears, and without any forensic evidence, Nick had his doubts. As he delved a little deeper it transpired that a neighbour had heard two women arguing in the house on the fateful night. And when Scott admitted that Sylvia had decided to leave him and return home, Jim's motive for murder disappeared. Nick was at a loss until it dawned on him that the only neighbour who hadn't mentioned hearing two women row was Anne Fowles. When he questioned her, she broke down and confessed. A fight had broken out after Sylvia had returned home to find Jim and Anne in each other's arms. Anne had pushed Sylvia to the floor and she had hit her head on the fireplace. Anne had used her own car to dump the body, and Jim had confessed to the crime in an effort to protect his lover.

## Nick's stalker

Being a local hero definitely has its drawbacks as Nick found out after rescuing Sandra Croft from her burning house. Later, when Nick visited her in hospital, she admitted that she was drunk

After rescuing Sandra Croft from a burning house, Nick was horrified to discover that she was stalking his every move. Eventually the obsessed Sandra realised the only way she would get Nick was to kill his girlfriend Jo.

when the fire started, having been drowning her sorrows over a broken love affair. Nick was suitably sympathetic. On being discharged from hospital, Sandra stayed at the Aidenfield Arms while her house was being repaired. It was the perfect spot for her to see her hero Nick again, but the sight of Jo with him did not please her. It wasn't long before she complained to the police that someone was following her and named her ex-boyfriend, Clive Kenway.

She turned up at the police station again to report that Kenway had stolen a gold bracelet from her house. Ventress was dispatched to Aidensfield to keep a lookout for Sandra's tormentor, but by now it was Nick who was starting to feel stalked by her, particularly when he discovered that Sandra had called at Jo's cottage on the pretext of borrowing water for her car radiator. Then, spotting Ventress on duty, she reacted angrily by ringing Nick at Jo's cottage and demanding that he alone guard her. Nick confided in Jo about his increasing concerns regarding Sandra's possessive behaviour, but Jo thought he was overreacting. Kenway painted a different picture, however, revealing that Sandra had behaved maliciously when he had ended their affair. Nick returned home to find Sandra waiting for him, playing with Katie. She said she wanted to drop the charges over the stolen bracelet. Nick told her to stop pestering him.

The next day Eileen discovered a gold bracelet in the pocket of Nick's old police jacket and, since it had just come back from the cleaners, she realised that Sandra must have planted the bracelet on her visit to the police house. Unaware that the bracelet had been found, the vengeful Sandra then accused Nick of stealing it and demanding that Blaketon search the police house. He disarmed her by returning the bracelet, which Nick had just handed in. He strongly advised her to leave Nick alone and asked Ventress to keep an eye on her.

But Sandra wasn't giving up without a fight. She went straight to Jo and told her that she and Nick were lovers. It took all of Nick's powers of persuasion to convince her that Sandra was lying.

However, Sandra had one last trick up her sleeve – murder. Biding her time, Sandra spotted her chance and drove her car at Jo. Spotting the danger, Nick pushed Jo out of the way, thereby placing himself in the path of the car. Happily, Ventress was in one of his more alert frames of mind and drove the police car in front of Sandra's, forcing her to stop. While Sandra was led away, a shaken Jo gladly accepted Nick's offer to stay with her overnight.

> **Did you know?**
> David Stockwell's clothes, might look like they've come from a charity shop, but they are made by a smart London tailor. He has been begging the costume department for some decent clothes since he became a regular in the show – with no success.

## Voices from the grave

All sorts of nasty little secrets were revealed in a rash of poison-pen letters. George received one regarding after-hours drinking and Ventress was sent a letter accusing him of receiving Cup Final tickets from a dubious source – namely

Greengrass. Then Maggie, too, received a letter, but of a more serious nature. She revealed to Nick that during nursing training she had embarked on an affair with a married man who went on to become a leading public figure. She became pregnant and had an illegal abortion. So distressed was she now that her secret was about to be made public that she crashed her car, but luckily escaped serious injury. Even Blaketon was sent a letter but he kept quiet about its contents.

Nick and Bellamy decided to pay Greengrass a visit to check the typefaces on a number of typewriters he had recently acquired. They found that one of the machines matched the typeface on the anonymous letters. Greengrass denied any involvement and, to prove his point, allowed Nick to read his own embarrassing letter. Ownership was traced back to the recently widowed Joyce Jowett. She told Nick that her husband became embittered when he was disqualified from his position as leader of the district council for a minor oversight and used to work off his anger by writing to other prominent members of the community about their own failings. She was horrified to learn that Thomas had instructed his solicitor to post the letters after his death.

The open moorland above Aidensfield provided no cover for villains to hide from the watchful eyes of the local constabulary.

## Bellamy smells something fishy

Ashfordly police were involved in a surveillance operation after a bank robber, Ronnie Savage, escaped from prison with the help of his brother-in-law, Bill Thompson. Blaketon briefed his men and showed them photographs of Ronnie and his wife Brenda. At the same time a pub run by Anne (Ronnie's sister) and Thompson was put under police observation. Nick, in plain clothes, saw Brenda and Thompson arrive at the pub by car and, joined by Bellamy, followed Brenda to Whitby, where they watched her meet a man at the docks. It was obvious that she was busy arranging Ronnie's escape by boat.

Inspector Jennings took charge of the operation and was told by Nick that Thompson's car had a tow bar attached, suggesting that Ronnie may be hiding in a caravan. Nick started working undercover as a labourer on the docks and realised that his supervisor, Penrice, was the man who had met with Brenda. There was a close call when Greengrass arrived at the docks to buy cut-price fish from Penrice, but backed out of the deal when he saw Nick working there. Fortunately, he didn't blow Nick's cover. Meanwhile, Bellamy was given the task of keeping watch at night but, when he spotted Thompson talking to a boat captain on the docks, there were no officers around to provide backup. Bellamy left his post to follow the pair and was rumbled by the boat crew and locked in the fish hold.

Nick reported Bellamy's disappearance to Blaketon, but Jennings refused to order a search for fear that it might jeopardise the operation. Jennings then questioned Greengrass about his connections with Penrice and in the course of the interview Greengrass mentioned a couple

*'Ventress manages to store information – he's like a smoking filing cabinet.'*
*– William Simons*

who were staying in a caravan. The police immediately raided the caravan, only to find that the occupants were naturists! Back in Whitby, Nick saw Ronnie Savage finally arrive at the docks. Nick followed him onto the boat and managed to raise the alarm, leading to the arrest of Savage, Thompson and Penrice. Bellamy was found in the hold – unharmed but reeking of cod.

## A tale of two Santas

Eileen was torn when her wartime sweetheart, Antonin, turned up in Aidensfield hoping to rekindle their romance. Although they hadn't met for 25 years, the old spark was still there. Antonin proposed and asked her to return to France with him. After much agonising, she decided she couldn't marry him because of her

Maggie, Eileen and Gina were roped in to supervise the play and the children had an unexpectedly large audience after a coachload of pensioners became stuck in snowdrifts and were taken to the relative warmth of the village hall. There was still one minor problem to be overcome. The children were hoping to meet Father Christmas, a role for which Ventress had been hand-picked. But he, too, was caught in the snow and so Greengrass was brought in as a last-minute replacement. Having battled his way through the drifts Ventress was not amused to find Greengrass ready to take his place.

Back at the cottage, the mood was turning romantic as Nick proposed to an ecstatic Jo. Everyone was delighted for them – except Jo's parents. For, when Nick asked Mr Weston for Jo's hand in marriage, Mrs Weston angrily

*Above:* Even Greengrass mucked in when snow drifts delayed Father Christmas.

*Right:* Festive spirit was in short supply when Ventress discovered that he had a rival Santa.

responsibility towards Katie. Antonin left, but he was to prove far more determined than Eileen had realised.

Meanwhile Jo and Nick were stranded in Jo's cottage by a fierce blizzard which raged on the day of the school's Nativity play.

objected to the union and the meeting ended in a blazing row. The path of true love was anything but smooth.

## The missing constable

Finding a load of pig manure dumped on his driveway, Special Constable Hector Cowley immediately suspected a local pig farmer, Betty Sutch, as the culprit and set off to confront her. There was a stand-up row, after which Hector mysteriously vanished. When he failed to turn up for morning traffic duty, Nick was sent to look for him. Hector's put-upon wife, Anthea, seemed unconcerned that she hadn't seen him since he went to call on Betty, but Nick found indications of something more sinister when he visited the Sutch farm. He noticed that Betty's son, Simon, was wearing a special constable's jacket with the initials 'HC' inside. At first, Simon claimed to have bought it from a second-hand shop, but then he admitted having found the jacket in a pig sty.

Blaketon ordered a thorough search of the Sutch farm, which unearthed more items of police uniform in a pig sty. Betty had no explanation apart from the fact that she had discovered someone else's wheelbarrow next to the pig sty. Macabre rumours began to circulate in the village about Hector's having been fed to the pigs, but Betty was able to produce a solid alibi for the night of his disappearance – she had spent it with her secret lover.

Nick relayed the news about the discovery of the uniform to Anthea and noticed that she had been burning a bundle of men's clothing in a garden incinerator. Anthea admitted to having had an argument with Hector but denied any

Betty Sutch (Julie T. Wallace) and her son, Simon, were at the centre of the riddle of a missing Special Constable.

knowledge of his whereabouts. However, she did confess to using the mystery wheelbarrow to dump his beloved police uniform in the pig sty. She was furious that Hector had gone on holiday with his sister without her, despite her objections. She had also deliberately forgotten to post Hector's letter to Blaketon, so Anthea's revenge got even sweeter when Hector faced Blaketon's wrath when he finally returned.

## The mugging of Granny Bellamy

Bellamy's granny had just moved into her new home and embarrassed him by bringing cakes into the police station. After withdrawing some money from the post office, she was followed home by Murray and Broadbent. Murray snatched the old lady's handbag and knocked her viciously to the ground. The likely suspects were Duster Murray and Red Broadbent who had been released after a previous mugging victim had been too scared to attend an identity parade.

Following the mugging of his grandmother, Bellamy admitted planting incriminating evidence on the chief suspect.

So, while Granny Bellamy was taken to hospital, Nick joined by an enraged Bellamy, searched Murray and Broadbent but found nothing incriminating. Then, during a second search, Nick was amazed to find Granny Bellamy's purse in Murray's pocket. In private, Bellamy admitted to planting the purse and asked Nick to alter his police notebook. It was not in Nick's nature to falsify evidence but Bellamy wouldn't back down.

When the case did come to court, Nick gave an uncharacteristically poor performance under cross-examination. Blaketon sensed that something was amiss and Bellamy was forced to confess that he had planted the evidence on Murray. The case was dismissed and a furious Blaketon threatened to report the two officers to headquarters. After much persuasion, the previous victim, Mrs Jackson, eventually relented and agreed to attend an identity parade. She picked out Murray, who reacted angrily, punching Ventress in the ensuing scuffle. Blaketon was delighted. Not only could he charge Murray with theft, but also with assaulting a police officer. What's more, he was able to tell Nick they were off the hook.

## Jo's heartbreak

Mrs Weston had still not reconciled herself to the prospect of her daughter's marriage to Nick. Her mood was not helped by the fact that she had been suffering from repeated headaches for which she had been recommended to see a neurologist. However, she stubbornly refused until Jo finally persuaded her to undergo tests at the hospital.

No sooner had Nick and Jo chosen an engagement ring than Jo's world was rocked by the sudden death of her mother from a brain haemorrhage.

But even there Mrs Weston continued to pour scorn on the forthcoming nuptials, causing yet another row with Jo. Not long after Jo had left, she received an urgent message to return to the hospital. Nick joined Jo just as her mother died from a cerebral haemorrhage.

Jo was devastated, fearing that the arguments over Nick may have brought on the haemorrhage. Her father also struggled to cope and became depressed. One day he headed off for a walk on the moors and went missing for hours. He later confided to Nick that he had wanted to commit suicide, but he was convinced the crisis was now past.

### Did you know?

Kazia Pelka has been a bridesmaid at two out of the five weddings that have taken place in Aidensfield. She claims that wedding scenes are the most tedious to shoot as there is so much hanging around – much like the real thing!

## In the doldrums

Greengrass thought all his Christmases had come at once when he met a wealthy young Australian couple, Len and Julie Wilcox, who were looking for ancestral family. When Len and Julie found their ancestors' gravestone, Greengrass, seeing pound signs flashing before his eyes, claimed he was a distant relative and did his best to persuade Len to buy local property so that he could manage it for them. The Australians were not impressed by the proposition. Undeterred, Greengrass tried a new tack and told them that he was related to aristocracy and was willing to sell them a number of priceless family heirlooms. When they expressed a vague interest, he rushed around buying antiques in readiness to pass them off as the family valuables. As Greengrass was about to congratulate himself on outsmarting the latest in a long line of mugs, he learned to his horror that the Wilcoxes had done a runner, taking with them an antique desk for which they hadn't paid him. Greengrass was highly indignant at having been conned.

The arrival of Claude's long-lost brother did not improve his mood, especially when he found himself caught in the middle of Cyril's marital dispute.

As if to reiterate that trouble comes in threes, Greengrass also became embroiled in a bitter feud over the secret recipe for the famous

> *'Visually Bernie and Greengrass are like Laurel and Hardy. There's big Greengrass and there's this little ferret running round after him.'*
> *– Peter Benson*

Aidensfield Buns. The original recipe was owned by a baker, Bill Dyson, who was now in a nursing home and refusing to reveal the contents, least of all to his warring sons Cliff and Frank. Bill was worried that his sons' refusal to work together would destroy the family business, so instead he wrote down the secret bun recipe and gave it to his old friend Greengrass for safekeeping. Greengrass got Eileen to bake a batch of buns and conducted an auction between the brothers. Resenting Greengrass's tactics, they joined forces to kidnap Alfred and said that they would hold the dog until Greengrass parted with the recipe. With matters threatening to get out of hand, Blaketon stepped in and supervised the exchange of Bill's recipe for Alfred. Bill then handed the recipe to both his sons, who immediately proceeded to wrestle for ownership, seemingly unaware that it was no longer a secret.

> ### Did you know?
> Nick Berry's head is such an odd shape that the costume designer never did manage to get his helmet to fit properly. In the end, Nick found it easier to just take it off.

# The great Aidensfield train robbery

After eleven-year-old Terry Ainsworth had been caught travelling on a train without a ticket, Nick called round to reprimand him. The boy's father, Eddie, had just been released from prison after serving ten years for armed robbery; his mother, Molly, worked as a machinist at De Vere's fur factory, where there had been a recent theft of offcuts. Suspicion had fallen on Molly, who was known to have been behind with the rent. Meanwhile, Terry was delighted when

Antonin in France, Jo had moved into the police house to look after Katie, but, when Blaketon came to hear about the arrangement, he told Nick that it was against police regulations. Before any action could be taken, there was a dramatic turn of events in the fur investigation. Ventress had tracked down a market trader selling fur offcuts. Steve Adams, who had been helping Gina at the pub now that George had been forced to retire through ill health, had bought her a pair of mink ear muffs from the market. Now Ventress was able to trace the

Young Terry Ainsworth (Oliver Peace) ultimately felt betrayed by his train robber father Eddie (James Gaddas). After showing Eddie his secret woodland den, the boy led the police there, too.

Eddie joined him on a local train trip and he showed his father his secret den in the woods. Nick was also on the receiving end of a reprimand – from Blaketon. With Eileen visiting

source back to the factory. Joyce, one of Molly's machinist colleagues, admitted having stolen the pelt so that she could lend Molly the rent money. Joyce also let slip that Eddie had been

Eddie Ainsworth was on the run after stealing a consignment of fur coats.

quizzing Molly about transport arrangements for a consignment of fur coats. It suddenly dawned on Nick that Eddie was planning to hold up the train. Jenkins, the factory manager, confirmed that the train carrying the coats had just left Aidensfield Station.

The police arrived just as Eddie and his gang were in the act of robbing the train. Unable to escape by car as planned, Eddie forced the driver to start up the train. Nick and Bellamy leaped aboard and chased the robbers through the train. Eddie's accomplices were caught but Eddie himself jumped off the moving train and hid in Terry's woodland den. Eddie told his son to get help from Molly, but the boy felt betrayed by his father, and, when Nick spotted him carrying a rucksack full of food, he persuaded Terry to take the police to the den.

### Did you know?

The biggest problem about playing a district nurse for Kazia was that she always had to look smart. If she was shooting a night scene in the cold, everyone else would go and have a sleep in the warm Land Rover, while Kazia had to sit primly so she didn't mess up her clothes and hair.

## Greengrass the gardener

More commonly known for being light-fingered rather than green-fingered, nevertheless Greengrass did the odd gardening job and agreed to clear undergrowth at the bottom of the Dobsons' garden. His enthusiasm for the project increased when Mrs Dobson happened

*'I wanted to make Greengrass a lovable rogue and most people like him in spite of his faults.'*

*– Bill Maynard*

Young Katie was the most important wedding guest when Nick and Jo tied the knot.

to mention that she had recently lost a diamond ring somewhere around there. Certain that Mrs Dobson would reward him handsomely for finding the ring, Greengrass borrowed a metal detector. He didn't find the ring but did unearth a Roman coin.

This whetted his appetite further still and, when the Dobsons went away for a few days, he persuaded Bernie Scripps to lend him a mechanical digger to speed up the hunt for the Roman coins. With no experience of using a digger, Greengrass cracked a water main in the middle of the Dobsons' lawn. The water board were summoned to help, leaving the Dobsons to return home to a scene of utter devastation. To complete Greengrass's misery, the water board workmen dug up a pot of Roman coins – which they promptly handed over to the Dobsons.

## Wedding bells

As Nick and Jo prepared for their wedding, two of their friends were undergoing different kinds of emotional torment. Gina, newly installed as licensee of the Aidensfield Arms, decided to end her brief relationship with the barman, Steve, after he had tried to undermine her by putting a pool table in the pub. To make matters worse, he had gone ahead and played in a pool match, despite having promised her that he wouldn't. Maggie received an even bigger shock when she learned that her estranged husband Neil was the new senior registrar at Ashfordly Hospital. It wasn't long before the pair were arguing over the treatment of a patient. In fact, it was just like old times. Later Neil tried to make Maggie discuss the sudden cot death of their baby four years

Friends and family saw Nick and Jo off on honeymoon following the reception at the Aidensfield Arms – an occasion marred by a brawl between Nick's grandfather and Greengrass.

previously – the root of the ill feeling between them. But Maggie told him icily that it was too late for them to comfort each other now.

Blaketon, too, was under duress. For months he had lived with rumours about administrative reorganisations or enforced early retirement, but now he was told that he had failed his medical owing to a heart condition. After 22 years' service, he couldn't imagine life outside the police.

## Did you know?

Nick Rowan's little two-stroke motorbike used to break down so often that it was constantly having to be pushed out of shot. In contrast, Mike Bradley's big butch motorbike has no such problems.

On the morning of his wedding day, Nick went for a drive on the moors to escape the chaos, only to be flagged down by Gwen Harding, who took him to the scene of an accident. The injured man, Ray Coombs, was in a highly agitated state, screaming that Gwen had tried to kill him. Gwen then jumped into Nick's MG and drove off, leaving Nick stranded with his wedding just a few hours away. Luckily, Nick managed to hail a passing van driver, who agreed to ferry Nick back into Aidensfield and take Ray to Ashfordly Hospital; but, when Ray's condition started to deteriorate, Nick decided to take him directly to hospital. Nick rang Bellamy – his best man – and Eileen from the hospital to say why he had been delayed.

Somehow, Nick made it to the church on time and everything went well, until Nick's grandfather and Greengrass had a scrap over the ownership of some jellied eels. Blaketon took charge and orderd them to leave. Peace reigned again, and the newlyweds set off on honeymoon but there was one more hurdle to overcome as Nick was stopped by the police for driving a stolen vehicle. He had forgotten to inform HQ that he had found his car!

Nick and Jo were all smiles following their wedding...little knowing that Nick would soon be stopped by the police.

# chapter 5

# Mike Roars Into Town

Mike Bradley roared into town like a bat out of hell. Dressed from head to toe in black leather, he rode his motorbike into Ashfordly at such a rate that Blaketon pulled him up for speeding. It was then that Blaketon learned that the long-haired young man before him was his new PC.

## Wild thing

Mike's introduction to village life could hardly have been more dramatic, as he found himself in the middle of a 'Bonnie and Clyde' wages snatch, which would leave his boss fighting for his life.

One of Gina's new initiatives was a morning sandwich run to the workmen at a pipeline compound high up on the moor. Greengrass had been making the daily deliveries but Gina, sensing that he was helping himself to some of the profits, decided to join him one morning. They set out in Greengrass's truck and on the way they spotted a hippie couple, Terry and Sharma Semple, who had been in the pub the previous evening. Terry told Greengrass that their car had overheated and asked for a lift. When Greengrass hesitated, Terry pulled a gun on him. The Semples jumped into the back of the truck, smashed the rear window, hid under the tarpaulin and, with a shotgun trained on Greengrass and Gina, told them to follow a security van to the compound. Meanwhile Mike, on his second day in the area, was on his way to the site as part of the regular patrols ordered for payroll delivery.

When the truck reached the compound, the robbers waited until the wages had been delivered to the site office. Once the security van had been driven off, they burst into the office, still holding Greengrass and Gina at gunpoint, and ordered the site manager, Corbett, to open the safe. To persuade him, Terry went outside and shot Greengrass's dog, and warned that Greengrass and Gina would be next. Corbett reluctantly opened the safe but, just as the Semples were about to make

New PC Mike Bradley's first encounter was with armed robber Sharma Semple (Eva Pope).

their getaway, they heard the sound of an approaching motorbike. Mike Bradley had arrived.

Corbett managed to indicate to Mike that something was amiss. Mike's suspicions were confirmed when he stepped outside and spotted the injured Alfred. Just then, unable to see Mike, Sharma emerged from her hiding place in the office. Sensing his opportunity, Corbett tried to overpower her but, as he crept towards her, a floorboard creaked and she turned round and shot him in the shoulder. Mike ran to the office, where he was felled by a blow from the butt of Terry's shotgun. He came round in time to see Greengrass's truck disappearing down the hill.

The Semples had immobilised the police bike and cut the telephone lines but Mike managed to repair the bike radio and tell Ventress about the raid, warning him that the robbers were driving Greengrass's truck. A mile down the road they switched to their Rover, leaving Greengrass and Gina shaken but unharmed and able to give the police a description of the Semples' car. Greengrass and Gina continued in hot pursuit, as did a posse of police vehicles, but Greengrass's knowledge of short cuts enabled him to catch the Rover. At the same time, Blaketon approached from the opposite direction. The Semples swerved off the road to avoid the police car and smashed into a huge boulder. Blaketon disarmed Terry and tried to pull Sharma from the burning car but the effort was too much for him and he sank to his knees, clutching his chest. He was having a heart attack. Greengrass carried Blaketon and Sharma clear of the car seconds before it exploded. While the robbers were led away, Blaketon was rushed to hospital. When he woke up in the ambulance, saw Greengrass next to him and heard that it was Greengrass who had saved his life, he nearly had another heart attack!

Blaketon recovered but Dr Neil Bolton told him that he would have to take early retirement from the police force because of his heart condition. Within three weeks he was running Aidensfield Post Office.

*'I don't know what they get up to in the Met, but up here we expect a copper to look like a copper, not a Roaring Stone'*
*– Blaketon's way of telling the new boy Mike Bradley to get his hair cut*

## Ventress goes missing

The Deightons, a notorious travelling family of tinkers, arrived in Aidensfield and provoked instant outrage from Jean Clarke, whose husband John, a former policeman, had been badly beaten up and left a physical wreck by the Deightons when he had attempted to arrest them for stealing. But, because there had been insufficient evidence to prosecute them, they had walked free. Pa Deighton was now hatching a plan to steal Alnwick Flyer, a well-known racehorse, and substitute for it a similar-looking horse for sale at auction. Ventress, who knew all about the Deightons' violent past, was determined to keep a close eye on the family.

At a local horse auction, Ventress and Mike observed Pa and Vinnie Deighton, plus their crony, Dermot O'Kane. Pa Deighton tried to buy a horse called Stonebreaker but was outbid by Greengrass, acting on behalf of a mystery buyer. Deighton did not take defeat kindly and resolved to steal Stonebreaker in the course of the night. Working

After his heart attack, Blaketon retired from the force to run the village Post Office.

alone, Ventress followed Pa Deighton to his secret camp in the woods while Vinnie and Dermot broke into Greengrass's barn and stole Stonebreaker. But Ventress's luck ran out when he was caught spying by the Deightons and imprisoned in a horse box.

Vinnie disposed of Ventress's car and, when Alf's wife reported him missing, Mike and Bellamy were sent to look for the Deightons. With Ventress still locked in the horse box, the Deightons successfully substituted Stonebreaker for Alnwick Flyer, but as they were doing so, Ventress managed to untie his bonds and escape by driving the horse box away. The Deightons gave chase but were captured at a police road block.

## Operation Gunsmoke

On his return from honeymoon, Nick was made up to acting sergeant, but shortly afterwards he lost the services of Eileen, who finally decided to move to France and marry Antonin.

One evening a fight broke out in the Aidensfield Arms, involving Keith Hibbert, manager of an auto spares business, his cousin Russell Palmer (a former racing driver) and a group of rugby players. Hibbert and Palmer were arrested and thrown in the cells, but during the night Palmer started shouting and, when Mike opened the cell door, he tried to escape. Mike manhandled him back in and Palmer hit his head on the wall. The next morning, he was found dead.

Dr Bolton noticed a cut and a bump on the head of the deceased. Hibbert, who had been in the adjoining cell, claimed that he heard Mike beating up Palmer in the night. Mike told Nick about Palmer's outburst and admitted that he may have hit his head on the cell wall. Mike was suspended from duty, but continued to protest his innocence. When his photo appeared in the local newspaper along with a story saying he was being put under investigation, the officer in charge, DI Shiner, agreed to his request to be moved to Scarborough pending the inquiry.

In the meantime, Nick not only discovered that Hibbert resented Palmer having a half-share in the business, but also that Palmer had been abroad recently and had been suffering from a fever. Although the preliminary tests indicated that Palmer had probably died from a blow to the head, the actual post-mortem revealed malaria to be the likely cause of death. In order to prove Mike's innocence, Dr Bolton advised Nick to trace Palmer's medication and, sure enough, Nick found the remains of a prescription bottle bearing Palmer's name hidden in the wastepaper bin in Hibbert's hotel room. Palmer had been shouting out for his

Celebrity Sightings – **Series Seven**
**Stratford Johns** played Greengrass's brother Cyril; and **Maggie Jones** (Blanche Hunt in **Coronation Street**) played Cyril's wife Edith; **Jeff Hordley** (**Emmerdale**'s bad boy, Cain Dingle) appeared as the train robber Mark Mullins, a member of the gang of Eddie Ainsworth, who in turn was played by **James Gaddas** (Vinny Sorrell from **Coronation Street**); **John Bardon** (EastEnders' Jim Branning) played Nick's brawling granddad at the wedding; **Frances de la Tour** guested as the aristocratic poacher, the Honourable Tessa Blundell; and **John Alderton** played the troubled ex-POW Jim Ryan.

Under a succession of licensees, the Aidensfield Arms ('played' by the real-life Goathland Hotel) has remained the focal point of village life.

medication but Hibbert had done nothing. Mike was reinstated but the police had only circumstantial evidence against Hibbert in connection with Palmer's death.

However, Mike wasn't off the hook yet. Shiner informed him that two criminals, Martin and Linden, whom Mike had helped put away while working undercover in London on 'Operation Gunsmoke', had just been released on appeal. As a result of the publicity over the death-in-custody case, they now knew where to find him. Mike needed to make a decision whether to move out of the area or sit tight.

His decision was partly influenced by the sudden arrival of Penny Gilbert and her baby son. Mike and Penny had been having an affair while he was working undercover on 'Operation Gunsmoke'. After he walked out on her a year ago, she had lost track of him until she saw his photograph in the papers. Mike was stunned to learn that six-month-old Thomas was his son. But, when Thomas became ill and was taken to hospital, Maggie learned that the boy was really only three months old. Gina, to whom Mike had already grown close, relayed the news to him and Penny admitted that he was not the boy's father. However, she threatened to tell Martin and Linden where to find him unless he paid her £400.

Mike sold his motorbike to raise the money and arranged a meeting place with Penny. But, when Martin and Linden appeared, he realised she had betrayed him. By now, Shiner had learned that Penny had been visiting Linden in

> *'Mike's a good contrast to Nick. He sees himself as a bit of an action man and likes to live fast – if you can live fast in Aidensfield!'*
> *– Jason Durr*

prison and, sensing that Mike could be in danger, he dispatched his men on the officer's trail. They arrived just as Martin was threatening to shoot Mike.

## New beginnings

After Nick and Jo had discussed making a fresh start elsewhere, he applied for details about employment with the Canadian police. To his delight, he was called for an interview with the recruitment board and offered a job.

While Nick and Jo started packing for the big move, two investigators from the Paranormal Research Institute arrived in Aidensfield to validate Clegghorn's haunted farm. Never one to pass up an opportunity to make some cash, Greengrass hijacked the investigators and told them that his own land was haunted by no fewer than three separate ghosts – those of Lady Ashfordly (the White Lady), a headless horseman and a mysterious dog known as the 'Ashfordly Hound'. The investigators felt obliged to check out the claims and so they waited until nightfall to

Jo receiving a farewell hug from Gina as she and Nick left Aidensfield to begin a new life in Canada. At their leaving party at the Aidensfield Arms the happy couple were presented with a goat!

witness the manifestation of the fearsome hound in the form of a glowing creature striding across Greengrass's top field. Given the official seal of approval, Greengrass opened his premises to the public and did a roaring trade. Visitors wishing to see the various apparitions were charged a shilling a head – except, of course, in the case of the headless horseman! However, Clegghorn was quietly seething at this blow to his own tourist

### Did you know?

When he was seventeen, Mark Jordon, who plays Bellamy, applied to join the police cadets just to please his mother – however, he deliberately failed the entrance exam so that he could become an actor.

attraction and exposed Greengrass to the investigators, revealing that the so-called 'Ashfordly Hound' was nothing spookier than Alfred wearing an old sack coated in luminous paint. The next day, Greengrass was besieged by angry punters demanding their money back.

After a hectic last day, which involved a post office robbery, Nick and Jo had a farewell party at the Aidensfield Arms. Their leaving present, rather bizarrely, was a goat. Needless to say, it didn't go with them!

## Saving Private Ryan

Recently widowed Jim Ryan was staying in Aidensfield as a guest of Blaketon. Ryan's behaviour became increasingly erratic and in the pub he got involved in a heated argument about the war and smashed someone's Japanese camera, as a result of which he was arrested by Mike. Blaketon explained that Ryan was a former Japanese prisoner-of-war who had suffered enormously working on the Burma–Siam railway. Blaketon agreed to replace the camera but Ryan's condition continued to give cause for concern. He told Dr Bolton that he needed to identify the enemy and then destroy him.

Ryan went AWOL for a period and skulked around on the moors, spying on Mike. While answering a hoax call regarding an accident on the moors, Mike was deliberately knocked off his bike. Dr Bolton reasoned that the trauma of his wife's death had caused Ryan to regress back to his POW days and see Mike as the enemy. When Blaketon returned home later that day, he found Ryan dressed in full commando gear. By now, the police were launching a desperate

Jo and Katie waving goodbye as their train sets off from Aidensfield station.

search for Ryan before he did serious damage. In the course of their moorland hunt they found Blaketon, bound and gagged. But there was no sign of Ryan... he was back at the police house waiting for Mike. When Mike arrived back at his house, Ryan launched into a frenzied attack. Luckily Maggie was not far behind and she managed to persuade the deranged soldier to turn himself in.

*'Mike's conscientious: he takes his job seriously but he likes to follow hunches, and he's also got his lighter side.'*
*– Jason Durr*

# chapter 6

# *Craddock: The New Broom*

Raymond Craddock, a Welshman who was Blaketon's replacement as sergeant at Ashfordly, was one of the old school. Vain, pompous and a stickler for rules and regulations, Craddock quickly set about trying to get his officers up to his own exacting standards. One look at Ventress told him that this would be the supreme challenge.

## Blaketon's dalliance

Much to everyone's surprise, Blaketon got into a spot of bother when his car was stolen from outside a house in Whitby. The car was found crashed and with a supply of drugs on board. Of course, Blaketon wasn't involved in anything illegal, but the house in Whitby belonged to a certain woman who just happened to be the wife of the local CID Inspector, proving that there was life in the old dog yet!

## Living in the Past

From the minute he started, Craddock set about trying to get his officers up to his own exacting standards. One look at Ventress told him that this would be the supreme challenge.

However, he did not have to wait long for a case that gave him the chance to demonstrate his powers of organisation and delegation. A full-scale nuclear alert on his patch – for Craddock it was a dream come true.

The drama began when a nuclear research scientist, Alec Formby, and his girlfriend Sonia stopped off for lunch at the Aidensfield Arms, leaving their Mini parked outside. When they came out again, they saw that the car had been stolen. Formby told the police that in the boot of the car, in a wooden box, was a radioactive atomic isotope, which, if removed from its protective lead casing, would cause death by irradiation. Craddock arranged for the BBC to broadcast a radio warning about the isotope and also enlisted the expert assistance of Roger Farrington from the Radiology Protection Service. Every police officer in the area was put on alert to look out for the missing Mini.

Welshman Raymond Craddock – the stiff new broom at Ashfordly police station.

Eventually, the car was reported to have been found, crashed in a country lane, but, by the time the police and Farrington arrived, it had vanished again. The driver was thought to

Trevor Chivers (Alan Halsall) showing off the stolen isotope to David Stockwell and Greengrass. Trevor's brother Stuart soon developed cold feet as the game threatened to get out of hand.

have been hurt in the crash and when Maggie saw William Reynolds, a known car thief, being treated for injuries at Ashfordly Hospital she notified the police. Reynolds admitted having stolen the Mini and said that it had been taken to Anderton's scrap yard in Aidensfield. At the yard, the police found the car but there was no sign of the isotope, which had been removed from its wooden box.

The lead flask had been taken from the car yard by two local youths, Trevor and Stuart Chivers, who were planning to sell it for scrap.

They tried to do a deal for the flask and some old copper with Greengrass, who put it in his shed and told them to come back later. But when Mike called at the school and described the isotope to the children, warning of the dangers of tampering with it, Trevor decided that after school he would fetch the isotope from Greengrass's shed and explode it in front of his mates. Greengrass, finding the shed empty, lost no time in telling the police. A worried Stuart told the police that Trevor intended to explode the isotope in front of his friends at a local landmark known as Sillers Drop. Seeing the police arrive in force, Trevor bolted, fell over the cliff edge and landed on a ledge. Mike was winched down to rescue him. Amazingly, the isotope was undamaged.

Elsewhere, Gina was hit by a double blow. First, Uncle George died, and then she went down with food poisoning caused by a batch of home-made horseradish sauce. Her Aunt Mary came to stay while she recuperated. While Mike was not happy to see Maggie move back in with her estranged husband, scuppering his own chances of romance with the district nurse. Dr Bolton had become the village GP by taking over the Aidensfield surgery, viewing the switch as a means of rekindling his relationship with Maggie. And Bellamy, thrown out of his lodgings, took up Mike's invitation to share the police house – which was very much against police regulations.

One popular decision on the part of Craddock was the appointment of Sue Driscoll as the station's clerical assistant. Bellamy was pariculary delighted and tried to ask her out on a date, but ended up agreeing to cook dinner for her, Gina and Mike. Not knowing an omelette from a casserole, he persuaded Gina's Aunt Mary to do the cooking and then passed it off as his own. Everyone was impressed – until Gina recognised it as being Mary's. Bellamy was getting nowhere fast.

## Greengrass in the mire

On a visit to a wealthy gardening client, Dorothea Cliveden, Greengrass was startled to see her with her face covered in green mud. After Gina had enlightened him about cosmetic mudpacks, Greengrass visualised definite money-making possibilities and tried to convince Mrs Cliveden that local Crackley Mire mud, which he would be only too happy to supply, was every bit as good for the skin as the expensive jars of Dead Sea mud that she used at present. He embroidered his presentation with the tale that Lady Ashfordly had discovered the youthful properties of Crackley Mire mud in the last century and that, although she was eighty when she died, she had looked more like a woman of forty. And that, claimed Greengrass, was down to the beneficial minerals in the mud.

Mrs Cliveden expressed an interest but stunned Greengrass by first asking for a sample to analyse. So he went out and bought a jar of Dead Sea mud and put it in a jar labelled Crackley Mire. Naturally, the laboratory gave the new mud a favourable report, as a result of which Mrs Cliveden ordered a number of jars from Greengrass. But when she took a bath in it, she developed a hideous skin rash. Greengrass muttered something about pollution and beat a hasty retreat.

### Did you know?

The first police station used in **Heartbeat** was in the middle of the village, but the noise from the market forced the team to build an exact replica further away. They now use a Citizens' Advice Bureau as the exterior – they couldn't use the interior as it is painted pink throughout!

It wasn't all plain sailing when estranged couple Neil and Maggie Bolton decided to make another go of things.

## Woman abducted

When Mike spotted Keith Winstanley acting suspiciously outside the surgery, he noted the registration number of the car that came to pick him up. Soon afterwards, Maggie and Neil reported a theft of drugs from the surgery. On the other side of the village Mel Drinkwater packed an overnight bag and told her mother that she was staying with her best friend, Karen Reilly. But Mel was secretly planning to elope to Gretna Green that night with her boyfriend, Terry Phillips. After meeting up with Karen, who gave her a wedding present, Mel set off for her rendezvous with Terry in a country lane. When Mel failed to turn up for work at Aidensfield Bakery the following morning, Mrs Drinkwater told her husband that she thought Mel had eloped with Terry. Nobody thought anything was amiss until Terry said that she hadn't been there when he had gone to pick her up. Everyone was concerned that she could have been abducted.

However, the first suspect, Mel's ex-boyfriend Michael Davies, had an alibi. But when Karen told Bellamy that Davies and his friend Keith Winstanley had once tried to spike her and Mel's wine, the police dug a bit deeper and found that Davies had a record for drug dealing and was also the owner of the car seen by Mike outside the surgery. Davies's alibi proved to be false, but, while he put up his hands to stealing the drugs, he denied having anything to do with Mel's kidnapping.

As the hunt intensified for the missing girl, Mike casually chatted to a bakery delivery man, Barry Hadfield. In the course of the conversation,

## Did you know?

When the truck containing the toxic waste blew up, the explosion was so large that car alarms started going off and the police received hundreds of calls from a concerned public. They were right to be concerned, as Jason Durr did injure himself as he jumped from the truck.

*'See, the difference between me and Blaketon, David, is that he's a bureaucrat, I'm a risk taker. He ends up behind a shop counter, I end up making a fortune. I mean, look at the two of us: who would you rather be?'*

*– Greengrass*

Hadfield dropped a ring box and said that he was engaged to a girl named Jeanie Walsh.

In the meantime, Maggie had become concerned when Hadfield had refused to see her husband about a bad headache. The Boltons decided to pay Hadfield a house visit. Thinking over what Hadfield had said to him, Mike found that 'Jeanie Walsh' was the name of a shop. Sue confirmed his suspicions by revealing that Hadfield had told her that his fiancée's name was Melanie. Maggie and Neil arrived at Hadfield's house to find Mike and Craddock already waiting. There was no sign that anybody had been in the house. Then Maggie remembered a farmhouse that had once been owned by Hadfield's parents. The four rushed there and found Hadfield and Mel. Hadfield was convinced that Mel loved him because she had once sent him a Valentine card. Poor Mel was so relieved to be released from her ordeal that she agreed to delay her wedding plans.

A lorry stuck under a low bridge threatened a major disaster for the villagers of Aidensfield.

## Passion killer

When Mike and Bellamy discovered a man's body lying in a gully on the road to Whitby, Dr Bolton was called out to give his opinion as to cause of death. He noticed that the victim had burn marks on his arm and that, bizarrely, his shoes were on the wrong feet. Craddock recognised the man's clothing as specialist cycling gear sold only in Italy, yet there was no sign of any bicycle. From the position of the body and the mystery of the shoes, Dr Bolton suggested that the victim may have died elsewhere and that the cause of death was probably not from a straightforward fall.

As deadly chemicals seeped from the truck, it was left to Mike to save the day by driving the vehicle clear of houses seconds before it exploded.

86

Assorted tyre tracks were found nearby and Mike recovered a piece of material snagged on a fence. Then Craddock spotted David Stockwell riding a racing bike and took him in for questioning. David's answers were typically confused but Greengrass threw more light on the matter when disclosing that he and David had found the bike abandoned on the moors.

Ventress pursued his enquiries at Phil Robinson's cycle shop and learned that Paolo Ermini, an Italian cyclist, had not been seen by his wife since the previous night. Paolo's wife, Lizzie, identified the body as that of her husband. Suspicion fell on a fellow cyclist, Tony Eccles, who had once been engaged to Lizzie, and was Paolo's bitter rival in the local cycling club; but another avenue of enquiry presented itself when Sue Driscoll revealed that her Aunt Millie, wife of Barry Watson, had been having an affair with Paolo.

Mike and Craddock matched the tyres of Barry's van to the tracks found near the body and the post-mortem confirmed that the corpse had been moved after death. The cause of death was a heart attack and the burns were found to have been made by an electric fire. Sue told Millie that Barry was in the frame for murder and he was subsequently brought in for questioning but said he had been playing in a darts match all evening. Unable to stand by and see her husband wrongly accused, Millie confessed that Paolo had suffered his fatal heart attack on her hearthrug during a passionate bout of lovemaking. He had burned his arm on her electric fire. In an attempt to make it look more like an accident, she had dressed him, put him and the bike into her husband's truck and driven up onto the moors.

## Mike to the rescue

Residents had been complaining about lorries making late-night deliveries to Colin Horton's newly opened factory, but the police said they

'When I turned up for my first read-through, everyone asked, "Are you playing the idiot?" I didn't take it personally.'
– David Lonsdale as David Stockwell

were powerless to act. So a group of pensioners – among them Granny Bellamy – formed a human barrier to prevent lorries entering the factory, whereupon Horton called the police. Horton insisted that the lorries were merely bringing in material to fill in old mine shafts in the factory grounds and Granny Bellamy was tactfully persuaded by Mike to stop the protest.

The following day dead fish were found in a stream passing close to the factory, but Horton vehemently denied using pesticides or dumping chemicals illegally. However, Mike received a tip-off that metal drums were stacked up in the factory yard. He tried to take a look around, only to be apprehended by security guards and ticked off by Craddock for acting without a warrant.

The police were called out again when Granny Bellamy handcuffed herself to the

Sgt. Craddock enjoying a rare moment of on-duty relaxation with Mike and Bellamy, but it wasn't long before he was wielding the big stick again.

factory gates. While Bellamy was dealing with his rebellious relative, Mike noticed a lorry loaded with drums inside the gates. He was about to question Horton when the factory owner drove the laden lorry out through the gates. His regular driver had refused to dump the remaining chemicals, leaving Horton to do his own dirty work, but, unsure of the route, he got the lorry wedged under a low bridge. The crushed drums started to leak. Mike was first on the scene and managed to free the lorry by deflating the tyres. He then drove the lorry into a field – well away from houses – and jumped clear seconds before the vehicle burst into flames and exploded.

A week later, Mike and Bellamy were on patrol when a young woman named Rachel Palmer told them that her sister Marianne had been attacked at her home, Elwood Grange. They found Marianne unconscious at the foot of the stairs and saw a man running off. Marianne's husband, David, was away at an auction, but

**Did you know?**

**Heartbeat** has been sold to more than thirty countries, from Norway to New Zealand, Slovenia to the Seychelles. It is so popular in Australia that, when the series is on air, the percentage of Australians visiting Whitby and North Yorkshire increases by 40 per cent.

> *'If Blaketon was a wooden club, Craddock is a rod of iron.'*
>
> *– Philip Franks*

when he returned he pointed the finger at a local character called Lenny, who lived in a nearby caravan, and whom he had recently sacked. David also stated that a gold locket was missing. When questioned, Lenny admitted having been in the house but said that he had found Marianne unconscious and had run away when he heard the police car arrive. The following day Marianne died and a distraught Rachel turned to Mike for comfort. With the case now a murder inquiry, Lenny was released on bail after a search of his caravan failed to unearth the missing locket.

Meanwhile, Mike and Rachel began to grow close. She started to confide in him, implying that David had financial problems and that more than a piece of jewellery had been taken. However, David was able to produce auction receipts to substantiate his alibi, which was also confirmed by his auctioneer's clerk, Kirsty Williams. Mike called on Rachel again after work and this time they ended up in a passionate embrace, but she became upset when he explained that further involvement with her would jeopardise the murder investigation. Craddock, too, suspected that Mike was getting too close to Rachel and sent him off on leave. When Bellamy caught them together at the police house, he packed Mike off to his Auntie Ida's B & B in Saltburn.

Back in Aidensfield, Maggie and Aunt Mary were planning a French theme party as a surprise for Gina, who was desperately looking for some excitement to spice up her life. Come the day of Gina's birthday, Mary hid all her cards and pretended that she hadn't remembered. A disconsolate Gina decided to take the day off.

With Mike out of the way, Craddock and DI Randall visited Rachel, who denied having said that more than one item of jewellery had gone missing. She accused David of having an affair with Kirsty. The police found David at Kirsty's house, where he explained that they were business partners, selling stolen antiques. But they weren't murderers. He admitted that he had slept with Rachel before marrying Marianne, as a result of which Rachel had developed an obsession for him. The police decided to pay a return visit to Rachel. She wsan't there, but they did find the gold locket along with other pieces of jewellery. Bellamy found evidence that Rachel had followed Mike to Saltburn.

Oblivious of what was happening in Aidensfield, Mike took a walk along the front at Saltburn and was delighted to bump into Gina. But Rachel was watching and, when she saw Mike give Gina a friendly kiss, she confronted him and accused him of using her. Rachel ran onto an unsafe section of the pier, followed by Mike, while Gina summoned help. Rachel told Mike that Marianne had fallen down the stairs during a fight she was having with her about David. Rachel became increasingly edgy, threatening to jump any moment, but, as she took a step back, Mike managed to grab her and pull her to safety. Reinforcements arrived and she was taken into custody. As for Gina, she arrived home just in time to miss her own birthday party!

# chapter 7

# Mike's Love Match

Jackie Lambert, Aidensfield's new solicitor, arrived to work for her uncle. Feisty and uncompromising, Jackie was keen to assert her independence and prove herself in her own right. This attitude caused more than a few explosive encounters with Mike, who couldn't help admiring her.

## A legal matter

When Peggy Tatton dug her heels in and refused to leave Deep Bank Farm after her brother's death, Mike met his match in Aidensfield's feisty new solicitor, Jackie Lambert.

Meanwhile, the Boltons' new-found solidarity suffered a hiccup when Neil was accused of indecently assaulting a patient, Elaine Aubrey, causing her car to crash. Neil was outraged, insisting that their relationship was purely professional, but Elaine produced a torn dress and details of Neil's past that made Maggie question whether her husband was telling the truth. However, closer investigation revealed that Elaine's real name was Mrs Davidson. Her husband, a doctor, had recently committed suicide. Suddenly it all became clear to Neil. Dr Davidson had been his mentor, but Neil had given evidence against him after an operation went wrong and a child had died. Dr Davidson had been disqualified as a result.

Elaine admitted that she was seeking to discredit Neil and, utterly distraught, she tried to jump in front of a train. The ever-alert Mike caught her just in time.

Solicitor Jackie Lambert quickly proved a force to be reckoned with, both at work and at play.

## The death of Neil Bolton

Discovering that she was four weeks pregnant, Maggie experienced mixed feelings. Neil suggested they go away to discuss the situation but she chose to join Gina on a weekend away instead. Neil was hurt by the exclusion but put on a brave face to wave Maggie and Gina off at the station.

In their absence, fire broke out at a house in Aidensfield. Neil, believing a toddler to be trapped in an upstairs bedroom, dived into the flames, unaware that the boy had already been rescued by his stepbrother. Mike raced to the scene and tried to climb a ladder to the window of the upstairs bedroom but, as he neared the top, a sudden explosion blew out the pane of glass. Neil's body was later recovered by the fire brigade. The fire had been started deliberately by the family's cash-strapped father, a struggling writer called Archie Roberts. Thinking that the house would be empty, he had hoped to cash in on the insurance.

Unaware of the tragic turn of events, Maggie told Gina that she had decided to return home early so she could tell Neil that she loved him and was really happy about being pregnant. Arriving back at the station full of optimism for the future, she was met by a grim-faced Mike, who broke the awful news.

and asking Terry to look after it. Terry maintained his innocence, adding that Rory Shaw, a punter who had bought Gina a drink, had also been sitting at the table. Mike had a word with DC Thomason, one of the investigating officers, who pointed out that only Gina had been caught with drugs during the

Dr Neil Bolton seeing Maggie off for a short break so that she could sort out her feelings about being pregnant. It was the last time she would see him alive.

## The framing of Gina

Egged on by her new manager Terry, Gina resumed her singing career in a Whitby nightclub but things turned sour when the club was raided by police and drugs were found in Gina's handbag. Gina said they must have been planted by someone and asked Mike for help. She remembered leaving her bag on the table

raid. Thomason told Mike that Terry was not a known dealer and that they were still looking for Rory. It was a bit of a surprise, then, when Mike saw Rory getting into Thomason's car outside the club.

Whitby CID eventually admitted that Rory was a police informer and because they still suspected him of dealing drugs, they had tipped him off about the raid. This time they raided the club unannounced and found Rory dealing in the main office. He tried to escape, but was apprehended by Mike. Tricked by Mike into thinking that he had left his fingerprints on the coating of the drugs, Terry admitted slipping the bottle into Gina's bag. The good news for Gina was that she was off the hook. The bad news was that she was left looking for a new manager.

---

### Did you know?

Kazia filmed her farewell scene before she had actually finished filming her other scenes. As a result, poor Kazia felt like she was leaving for about six weeks, and with every set bringing back happy memories, she was tearful for the rest of her time on the show.

---

## D-Day for Mike

It was never going to be easy for Mike and Jackie to separate their professional and private lives, but their conflicting interests came to a head when her Uncle Henry accidentally knocked a teenage cyclist off his bike. Seeing David Stockwell approaching, Henry panicked and drove off, leaving the boy lying unconscious in the road. Fortunately the victim escaped serious injury and David was able to give Mike a description of the car, along with part of its registration – HAJ.

Sifting through registration records, Mike and Bellamy found three cars that fitted the bill, and, since one belonged to Henry Tompkinson, Craddock suggested Mike should tactfully question him. However, Henry had gone home with flu and his wife, Joyce, stated that he had been playing golf with Blaketon earlier that day but had been at home with her at the time of the hit-and-run. When it emerged that neither of the other two suspect vehicles could have been involved in the incident, the net closed in on Henry, to the disgust of Jackie, who stormed out of the pub after a furious row with Mike about the case.

When Craddock and Mike caught up with Henry, he questioned the reliability of David as a witness. Jackie still refused to believe that

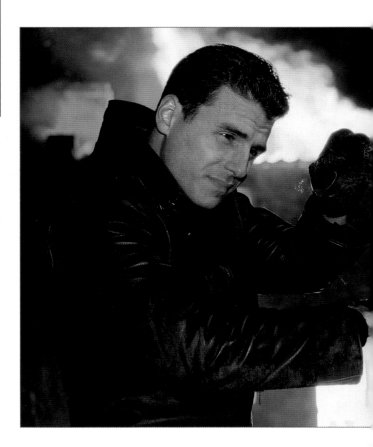

Despite his valiant efforts, Mike was unable to rescue Neil from the raging inferno.

Joyce. Jackie visited May Hawkins and found that Henry's leaving time put him firmly in the frame for the hit-and-run. Finally, he admitted to Jackie that he had knocked the boy off the bicycle. Joyce tried to blackmail Jackie into persuading Mike to drop his enquiries.

When Jackie learned about Mike's job application, she was shocked and felt that she had driven him away. She persuaded Henry to confess to the police but during the interview Craddock heard that Henry's car had not been damaged in the accident but had been scratched a few days later. Craddock promptly accused Rodney of fabricating evidence and revealed that he had just learned that Rodney's team at the Met had been suspended on corruption charges. The news came as a bombshell to Mike, who decided to withdraw his transfer application.

her uncle was guilty even though Blaketon had admitted that Henry might have been drinking and driving. Meanwhile, Mike's friend from London, Rodney, had arrived in Aidensfield, urging Mike to apply for a job with the Met. In the wake of his talk with Rodney and Jackie's outburst, Mike decided that he did want to apply for a job with the Met. Rodney then showed Mike and Craddock some flakes of paint, allegedly taken from the handlebars of the boy's bicycle, which matched damage to Henry's car.

Chatting in confidence with Jackie, Henry let it slip that he had visited a dying client, Sam Hawkins, on the afternoon of the accident – a statement that conflicted with that of his wife

*'Jackie and Mike certainly have their moments. They are both determined professionals with fiery spirits.'*
– *Jason Durr*

## A face from the past

Gina was surprised to see an old boyfriend, Terry Noble, who had gone AWOL from the army. Unaware of the seriousness of his crime – he had knifed a soldier during a card game – she smuggled food out of the pub to the derelict cottage in which he was hiding. But, when he asked her for money, she decided not to help him any more.

Alerted by the military police that Noble may be in the area, Ashfordly police stepped up their hunt for him, all the more so when his victim died from the stab wounds. Without Gina's assistance, Noble became desperate, broke into Colonel Hal Clifford's house and held the old war hero at gunpoint. Learning that Noble was wanted for murder, Gina told Mike about his cottage hideout, but a police raid found nothing. Meanwhile, Bellamy had cause to call on Colonel Clifford, who, with Noble threatening to shoot his dog, tried to get rid of Bellamy without arousing suspicion.

Bellamy spotted the disconnected telephone and crept round to the back of the house, but Noble had guessed what he was up to and knocked him out, hiding Bellamy's car in the garage. Noble's plan was to leave in the colonel's car so the wily old war horse persuaded Noble to wait until dark before he left. The clever colonel knew that, because he was only allowed to drive during the day due to cataracts, his car would be noticed if it was out at night. Sure enough, as Noble drove through Aidensfield wearing the colonel's hat and coat, Mike spotted the car and gave chase. He was eventually stopped by the military police and surrendered without a struggle.

While Gina was still coming to terms with the fact that her ex-boyfriend was a killer, there was another shock for her when Blaketon announced himself as the new owner of the Aidensfield Arms.

## Dirty tricks

One day Craddock's wife Penny received a visit from a couple of 'cowboys', Danny and Jimmy, who told her that her guttering needed cleaning. Greengrass watched the pair at work and saw them deliberately block the guttering before calling on the unsuspecting house owner. So, when Danny and Jimmy were put out of circulation, he tried to cash in on their little scam. Unfortunately, Craddock was wise to it and ordered Greengrass to clear all the blocked gutters in Aidensfield.

Bored with running the Post Office, Oscar Blaketon surprised everyone by buying the Aidensfield Arms.

Next, Greengrass crossed swords with Blaketon, who was standing at the local election, backed by Maggie. Greengrass and Bernie were supporting a rival candidate, Drabble, in the expectation that once elected a district councillor he would grant permission for a car and caravan park to be built on some waste ground – a project close to Greengrass's wallet. The campaign turned ugly with Greengrass tearing down Blaketon's posters and Blaketon sticking his own posters over Drabble's. Mike had to intervene when Blaketon, Greengrass and Drabble got into a heated argument, but Blaketon had one more trick up his sleeve, and he reminded Ventress about a fraud case in which Drabble had been found not guilty, although his partner, Payntor, had received a prison sentence.

When Blaketon heard from Bellamy that Drabble was now having an affair with Payntor's wife, he persuaded Payntor to make a signed statement implicating Drabble in the fraud case. Ventress tipped off the returning officer that Drabble was wanted by the police, enabling Blaketon to be elected councillor on the toss of a coin. Poor old Greengrass lost on all counts – his hopes of planning permission and his deposit money.

While Aidensfield was gripped by election fever, the celebrated novelist Honor Gale rented Whisper Cottage. Honor was excited to learn that Mike was the village policeman and called him out to the cottage on the pretext that her cat was stuck up a tree. A party of Borstal boys were also working in the area and, during a lunch break, one of them, Sloper, broke into Honor's cottage, where she cooked a meal for him and secretly recorded his conversation about his criminal background as the basis for a future book.

When Mike was summoned to rescue a walker in difficulty on Bleakedge, he discovered that it was Honor. He rescued her, but was unaware that a photographer was taking pictures. When the picture appeared in the local paper, Mike accused Honor of engineering a publicity stunt.

Action man Mike Bradley needed all his inner strength to handle a relationship with Jackie Lambert.

Back with the Borstal party, Sloper boasted to his mate Varley about his visit to Honor's cottage. Varley decided to try it, too, and broke into the cottage. Spotting signs of an intruder, Honor called Mike, but she'd cried wolf once too often and he refused to respond. As a menacing, drunken Varley cut the telephone wires, Honor managed to escape. Jackie then turned up at the cottage on a social visit and was chased into the woods by Varley. Hearing from the prison officer in charge of the Borstal party that Varley had absconded and remembering Honor's call about an intruder, Mike dashed to the cottage and was terrified to see Jackie's car outside. After finding the cottage deserted, he followed Varley's trail on his bike and managed to find Jackie before she came to any serious harm. The experience brought Mike and Jackie closer than ever and back at the cottage he proposed to her.

## More wedding bells

Mike and Jackie opted for a secret wedding at a register office with Bellamy as best man. However, things did not go smoothly as Maggie overheard the plans and inadvertently told Jackie's Aunt Joyce. Aunt Joyce was furious and refused to attend until talked round by Blaketon. However, that was the least of their worries. As befits a *Heartbeat* wedding, the groom very nearly didn't make it. Mike found himself held at gunpoint by a wounded train robber who had just been part of a £200,000 raid in which a signalman was shot. The robber was amused to learn that Mike was due to marry a solicitor, but Mike persuaded him to

After being held at gunpoint by an armed robber, Mike only just made it to the register office in time to marry Jackie.

### Did you know?

Jason Durr nearly died as he was getting changed in the back of a speeding car on the way to the wedding. He accidentally knocked the door handle with his elbow and flew out of the door! Mark Jordon hauled him back in just in time. The director was so pleased with the effect that he kept it in.

surrender by telling him that the signalman was out of danger. Rushing to the register office, he and Jackie found all their friends, including Joyce, waiting for them in a huge marquee.

The cake had hardly been cut before the newlyweds were at each other's throats. Investigating a car that had crashed into an Ashfordly tailor's shop window late one evening, Mike was horrified to learn that the suspect, Sean Banks, a photographer with a record for possession of drugs, said that he had been with Jackie at the time of the incident. Jackie started behaving oddly and confirmed Sean's alibi but refused to tell Mike why she had met him on two separate occasions.

Then Mike found an envelope containing explicit nude shots of a younger Jackie. He confronted her with them just as she was about to go into court before storming off. Eventually returning home, he was met by Jackie's lookalike sister Elizabeth, a vicar's wife who explained that she was being blackmailed for £1,000 by Sean over some

> *'Jackie's relationship with Mike took her by surprise. It was absolutely not what she was intending. She was coming to Aidensfield purely to work, to get some experience and then probably move back to London. She certainly wasn't coming to the middle of nowhere to fall in love.'*
> *– Fiona Dolman*

nude photographs he had taken of her during their distant affair. Jackie was acting as her intermediary. Fully briefed, Mike was able to set Sean up and have him arrested for demanding money with menaces. But this was just a taster of the tempestuous times ahead for the Bradleys.

## Alfred's identity parade

While Greengrass hired out his field for lurcher racing in partnership with Frank Pargoe, he was also being pursued by Mr Piggot from the council, who wished to discuss the rate revaluation of his property. Realising that Pargoe has been spotted by the ever-vigilant Blaketon, Greengrass feared that the police might put a stop to the racing, so he created a diversion by anonymously calling Ashfordly

---

**Celebrity Sightings – Series Nine**
The singer **Charlotte Church** made her acting debut as Katie Kendall in the 1999 Christmas episode 'Stag At Bay';
**Joe McGann** appeared as the shady artist Joe Vaughan in 'For Art's Sake'; and the former Take That star **Gary Barlow** played the pub singer Micky Shannon in the 150th episode of **Heartbeat**, 'The Son-In-Law'.

Hall to say that lurcher racing would take place illegally on His Lordship's land during a pheasant shoot.

After Greengrass and Pargoe had been warned by the police to stay away from Ashfordly Hall, Piggot eventually caught up with Greengrass, only to be bitten by his dog. Piggot reported the savaging to the police, giving Ventress the opportunity to impound all local lurchers until Lord Ashfordly's shoot was over. Acting on Greengrass's behalf, Jackie objected and, when Piggot was unable to pick out the culprit at a canine identity parade, the dogs were released. As the police continued to watch Lord Ashfordly's estate, the racing went ahead at Greengrass's place, with Claude raking in the money when Pargoe's lurcher won every race. But Greengrass didn't get much chance to spend it since Piggot exacted his revenge by charging a hefty business rate on Greengrass's property.

## Gina's love rat

Gina's latest boyfriend, Andy Ryan, was a deep-sea diver who broke her heart by heading off to Spain but won it back again by buying her a second-hand Mini Cooper on his return. At first he seemed happy helping out behind the bar, but he grew increasingly restless, disappearing for periods at a time. He told

Alfred may have stuck out like a sore thumb at the canine identity parade but he was released shortly afterwards without charge. However Greengrass's relief was to prove short-lived.

*'Even though Blaketon is involved with the community as a local councillor I think he'd love to set up his own private detective agency. Once a copper, always a copper.'*
– *Derek Fowld*

Mike that on one such assignation he had visited another girlfriend in Grimsby. Then Andy informed Gina that he was going to Scotland on business but Blaketon overheard him arranging to meet a friend near Scarborough. Blaketon followed him and discovered that Andy had a wife in Grimsby. When Andy came back to Aidensfield, having celebrated his anniversary, ready to pick up the reins with Gina, Blaketon confronted him and strongly advised him to leave the area. Gina was distraught until Blaketon told her the truth.

She thought that was the last she'd seen of Andy, but he reappeared a couple of weeks later and rescued a man who had jumped from Saltburn Pier. Impressed with his bravery, Andy spotted his chance and assured Gina that his marriage had been a mistake and that there were no children. But once again Gina was to be let down, when he suffered a ruptured spleen and named Gina as his next of kin, Blaketon felt it necessary to inform Mrs Ryan. At the hospital, Gina came face to face with Andy's wife and three children. Undeterred, he later told Gina that he was divorcing his wife and setting up a diving school in the West Indies. Even Gina couldn't fool herself any further and she finally got rid of him for good.

## Baby snatch

As a single mother, Maggie Bolton had not found it easy bringing up baby Sam. The demands of juggling a career and parenthood left her with precious little social life, so when Craddock, who was going through a rocky patch in his marriage, invited her to go ballroom dancing, she gladly accepted. But her hopes for a pleasant evening of dancing soon proved a trifle optimistic.

It all started when Roy Brooks, himself a single father of four, received a suspended prison sentence for horse theft. He was warned that, if he landed in any more trouble, his children would be placed in care. Shortly afterwards, he was taken in for questioning following the theft of a valuable racehorse from Lord Ashfordly. Crucial evidence against Roy was supplied unwittingly by Maggie Roy when her car was run off the road by his lorry. Jackie secured Roy's speedy release but, depressed by

> ### Did you know?
> Since it started in 1992, Heartbeat has had 5 producers, 40 directors, 53 writers, 5 births, 4 marriages, 26 deaths, 6 murders, 12 fires and 3 Alfreds! And let's not forget that of the 26 deaths, 3 of them have been Aidensfield's doctors. Here's hoping that Dr Tricia Summerbee bucks the trend!

With his marriage going through a bumpy period, Craddock invited Maggie to go ballroom dancing. A place on 'Come Dancing' surely beckoned...if only Maggie had been willing to sew all her own sequins.

being in trouble again, he went off on a drinking binge before finally walking out on his family. Christine, his eldest daughter, discovered Maggie's involvement and accused her of prompting Roy's latest breakdown.

Meanwhile, Maggie had struck up a friendship with a homeless woman, Brenda, whose son had died some years ago. But Maggie became concerned when Brenda began to take an unhealthy interest in Sam and turned down her offer to babysit while she went out with Craddock. Instead, Maggie hired Bellamy, who fell asleep and woke to find that that Sam had been taken from his cot. On her way home, a frantic Maggie remembered that Brenda had told her about her young son's death and named her as chief suspect. The police found

Sam's shawl in Brenda's empty cottage but there was no sign of either Brenda or Sam. Eventually, Brenda was found and she admitted taking the shawl but denied snatching Sam. It was Bellamy who made up for his terrible lapse when he found a drunken Roy and through him he learned that it was Christine who had taken Sam to get back at Maggie. The ordeal ended happily with Maggie being reunited with Sam and Roy resolving to be a better father.

## Greengrass shot

A car was found dumped in the river one night minus all its hubcaps. According to Grimsby police, it had been stolen from a ferry from Amsterdam and was the property of Archie and Marion Drew. When the Drews arrived to see their car winched from the river, they seemed strangely perturbed that the hubcaps were missing.

On the night that the car was dumped, Greengrass and David gave a lift to hitchhiker Micky Shannon, who booked into the Aidensfield Arms, telling Blaketon and Gina that he was a musician and used to play in an unsuccessful band. On the rebound from Andy,

**Did you know?**

When Tricia Penrose was called for her audition for the part of Gina, she was told to dress like Aveline from **Bread**. So she back-combed her hair, put on loads of make-up and a little short skirt. The next thing she knew, she'd got the job.

Having been shot by irate diamond smuggler Marion Drew, a wounded Greengrass was rushed to hospital by singer/crook Micky Shannon (Gary Barlow). The former Take That star was appearing in the 150th episode of Heartbeat.

Gina took an interest in Micky and persuaded him to play the piano and sing at the pub's music night.

Micky was a man of many talents and he had a proposition for Greengrass involving the growth of rare tree orchids from seed. Greengrass agreed to grow the seeds in return for a share of the eventual profits.

Shortly after, David recovered a car hubcap covered in axle grease, and then Blaketon disturbed an intruder in the pub and was knocked unconscious. Gina noticed that Micky had gone and that his room had been ransacked. In a drawer Mike found a T-shirt from Amsterdam, smeared in axle grease, and came to the conclusion that Micky had stolen the Drews' car because he had learned that they were smuggling valuables in the hubcaps. Now the Drews were trying to retrieve the goods from Micky.

Greengrass and Micky drove across the moors, hotly pursued by the Drews, who eventually forced them to a halt. The Drews demanded the return of their property and, when Greengrass tried to overpower Marion Drew, she shot him. In the commotion, Micky knocked out Archie and rushed Greengrass to hospital. The police arrived on the scene not long after Micky and Greengrass had left and arrested the Drews. Searching for Micky, Mike headed for Greengrass's place, where David revealed that Alfred had been behaving strangely after eating the orchid seeds. Mike inspected the seeds and realised they were marijuana. The lurcher was living up to the name of his breed. Shortly afterwards, Micky arrived to find Mike waiting.

Mike asked for the goods he had stolen from the Drews' car and Micky produced a bag of uncut diamonds. As a gesture of goodwill, Mike allowed

*'I'm telling you, Greengrass, one day your luck's going to run out. And on that day I'll be there.'*

*– Craddock*

Micky to play one last gig at the pub before being taken into custody.

In the meantime, Mike met Jackie's parents, Edwina and Lionel, for the first time. Jackie had omitted to tell them that he was a police constable and her mother made no attempt to hide the fact that she disapproved both of Mike's job and the police accommodation. Furthermore, she wanted Jackie to take a job in South Africa. Jackie was sorely tempted but decided that her place was with Mike.

## Jackie in jeopardy

Mike's jealousy continued to cause problems in his marriage. In his eyes every client of Jackie's was a potential lover. Over a period of days he and Jackie were plagued by a series of silent, early-morning telephone calls and Mike found a glove and some empty film wrappers dropped in the garden of the police house. When Jackie opened her diary and found the words 'I'm waiting' scrawled inside, Mike realised that Jackie was the target of the mystery caller.

Then, returning to the police house one

afternoon, he found a bouquet of red roses addressed to Jackie. In a jealous rage, he found out from the florist that they had been sent by Anthony Smythe, a solicitor and an ex-boyfriend of Jackie's. Mike made a bad situation worse by suggesting that Smythe was the prowler.

Behaving like the paranoid husband he was, Mike searched through Jackie's coat pockets and discovered a restaurant bill for

> *'Mike and Jackie clashed at first and she saw him as being a bit of a village cop and stuck in his ways, but, the more they came into contact, the more she saw his sparkle.'*
> *– Fiona Dolman*

two. Jackie admitted having had a meal with Smythe but was furious when Mike accused her of having an affair. She maintained that she was merely offering Smythe support while he was nursing his sick father, but Mike stormed round to Smythe's house and the two men ended up fighting. While Mike was out, Jackie spotted a man in the front garden. Still wearing her dressing gown, she ran out of the back door, and didn't stop until she reached the safety of the Aidensfield Arms.

Craddock took Mike off the case, leaving the investigation in the capable hands of

Jackie's marriage to Mike was a tempestuous affair, punctuated by his frequent bouts of jealousy.

Ventress, who decided to tap Blaketon's memory. Sifting through Jackie's court cases, Blaketon recognised the name of Martin Padmore, a bank employee who had been under suspicion of phoning and following a woman back in 1958. Mike and Ventress set off to question Padmore and, finding nobody at home, broke into his house. The living room was a shrine dedicated to Jackie; in a drawer was an empty revolver holster. Mike dashed to Jackie's office but learned that she had already left for home, unaware that Padmore was lurking in the back of her car. Partway through her journey, Padmore emerged from his hiding place and ordered her at gunpoint to drive to the moors. Having slammed on the brakes, she managed to escape from the car and run into the woods. Mike and Ventress spotted her car and heard her screams, and, when they arrived on the scene, Jackie succeeded in disarming the momentarily distracted Padmore. As Jackie's tormentor was taken into custody awaiting psychiatric reports, Mike made a resolution to be more trusting of his wife in future.

## Maggie leaves Aidensfield

Any prospect of a romance between Maggie and Graham Rysinski looked remote at first. Graham's mother Molly was terminally ill and Maggie knew that her dearest wish was to leave hospital and die in her favourite place. Graham was equally adamant that his mother should remain in hospital, but he could do nothing to prevent Molly discharging herself and fulfilling her wishes. In the end he realised that he had been wrong and was at his mother's side as she passed away peacefully.

With his marriage in turmoil, Mike was sad to see Maggie leave Aidensfield. He had been a great comfort to her since Neil's death.

Bellamy, Gina, Blaketon, Mike, Jackie, Ventress and the rest of the village turned out to say goodbye to popular district nurse Maggie Bolton.

### Did you know?

The first series of **Heartbeat** was shown on Friday evenings so there was quite a bit of swearing involved. By the second series, the cast had to clean up their act as there is now no swearing allowed on **Heartbeat** at all.

Maggie was touched when Graham gave her a piece of jewellery belonging to her mother. He then sent her flowers and invited her and Sam away for a weekend. Maggie accepted but soon realised that they were both too forthright to be compatible. They split up and Maggie left the village for a job at a hospital – but only after a surprise farewell party at the Aidensfield Arms.

# Blaketon's beauty

Blaketon received a surprise visitor in the pleasant shape of an old flame, Ursula Donne, who was back in Aidensfield after a spell in America. She told Blaketon that she was a widow now but his hopes of romance were swiftly shattered when Lord Ashfordly turned up and took her off for a day at the races. Blaketon recalled how devastated Ursula had been when Lord Ashfordly ended their affair years earlier. Lord Ashfordly then met Ursula for a drink at Webster's Hotel, an establishment that, she revealed, was owned by an American consortium in which she had inherited a major shareholding. Blaketon, too, arranged lunch with Ursula at her hotel, only to be stood up in favour of Lord Ashfordly.

Later, Lord Ashfordly confided to Blaketon that he was planning to invest in Ursula's latest hotel venture. Ursula's consortium was also developing Thornby Manor but, strangely, when Blaketon expressed an interest in making a financial commitment, Ursula told him that they weren't taking on new investors.

Blaketon began to smell a rat and asked Ventress to make discreet enquiries. They confirmed his worst fears but he arrived just too late to prevent Lord Ashfordly handing over a large sum of cash to Ursula, who promptly did a runner. Hell hath no fury like a woman scorned.

Lord Ashfordly and Blaketon found themselves rivals for the hand of old flame Ursula Donne (Sharon Maughan)...little suspecting that she was a con woman.

# chapter 8

# Greengrass's Successor

When Greengrass went to live with his sister in the West Indies, any hopes that Aidensfield's crime figures would plummet were dashed when Bernie Scripps's estranged half-brother Vernon turned up. Trouble followed Vernon around with a stalker-like zeal, and when Vernon decided to move into Greengrass's old house, it was as if Greengrass had never left!

Vernon Scripps's unexpected arrival in Aidensfield brought nothing but misery for half-brother Bernie, leaving the local undertaker looking more mournful than usual.

## I've Been a Bad, Bad Boy

Vernon quickly made his mark. With Bernie away for a few days, he and David Stockwell agreed to replace the fuel tank in Lord Ashfordly's Bentley in time for his niece's wedding but, to Vernon's dismay, David stripped the entire engine. They managed to repair the damage but, in doing so, left out a jubilee clip, with the result that Lord Ashfordly's car broke down on the way to the church. Bernie felt obliged to offer a replacement vehicle, and so it was that Lord Ashfordly's niece arrived at church for the happiest day of her life in a hearse!

## A family affair

Jacob Fairbrother, a quarry worker, was worried when his boss, Joe Henderson, delayed the repair of a faulty shutter guard on a stone-crushing machine. Joe and his wife Shona were entertaining Jackie's mother Edwina. Jackie was invited for dinner, too, but, when Mike arrived late, he noticed that no place had been set for him. Where Jackie's family were concerned, some things never changed.

The evening was interrupted when Joe received a call to say that there had been an accident at the quarry. Jacob was trapped by falling stones and Mike risked his own life to crawl into the debris and pull him to safety in the nick of time. Jacob's wife Pamela blamed Joe Henderson for the accident and asked Jackie to bring a case of criminal negligence against him. Edwina then asked Jackie to defend Joe and was livid to learn that she had already agreed to act for the other side. Shona suggested that Joe should pay Jacob some form of compensation but he refused point-blank on the grounds that it was tantamount to admitting liability.

Against the advice of Dr Tricia Summerbee, the young intern at Ashfordly Hospital, Jacob checked himself out of the ward and went up to the quarry to confront Joe. Mike was called out to defuse a potentially explosive quarrel, which ended with the two men exchanging threats. Jacob stormed off to see Shona and, forcing his way into the house, demanded his back wages. Returning shortly afterwards, Edwina found Shona lying dead on the living room floor. Joe said that he had last seen his wife late that morning before attending a Rotarian meeting in Whitby, while Jacob denied having gone to the Henderson house at all. Jacob was taken to the police station to make a statement but escaped when Vernon Scripps's electrical skills plunged the whole of Ashfordly into darkness.

With Jackie begging Jacob to turn himself in, Dr Summerbee told Mike that Shona, calling herself 'Jane Brownlow', had twice been treated at the hospital for mystery bruising. Jacob finally returned to the police station and admitted having visited Shona to demand his wages but maintained that she had been alive when he left.

Meanwhile, Ventress found out that Joe had lied about his arrival time at the Rotarian meeting and Edwina noticed that Joe was

*'If Vernon thinks there's a shilling to be made, he'll do anything.'*
*– Geoffrey Hughes*

behaving strangely and trying to keep her away from a bonfire in the garden. When he was taken away by Mike for further questioning, she found pieces of Joe's bloodstained shirt in the bonfire and told the police. Joe confessed that he had killed his wife in a rage after finding out that she had paid Jacob his wages.

## Bellamy's resignation

Bellamy and Gina had always been good friends but he never thought he was in with a chance until she kissed him tenderly after he had sorted

> ## Celebrity Sightings – **Series Ten**
> **David Essex** played the charismatic traveller Johnny Lee, who unwittingly brought a dangerous criminal to Aidensfield; **Russ Abbot** appeared as the self-styled entertainment legend Stanley Leroy; **Jean Alexander** played an elderly farming widow; and **Sharon Maughan** guested as the con woman Ursula Donne, an old flame of both Blaketon and Lord Ashfordly.

reinforced those sentiments while reprimanding Bellamy for his increasingly sloppy timekeeping. After a pregnancy scare, Bellamy decided that love was more important than his job and handed his resignation to Craddock, thinking he could become a double-glazing salesman instead.

Bellamy's next step was the proposal. He went out and bought an engagement ring and laid on a romantic scenario, which Gina would surely have found impossible to resist. His only mistake was in hiring Bernie Scripps to take Gina to the rendezvous. Bernie delegated the job to David, who was meant to take her to the ruins of Whitby Abbey, where, unbeknown to her, Bellamy was waiting with flowers, champagne and a soppy smile. But David took her to the Abbey Arms, a seedy pub in Whitby. She waited impatiently for over an hour before storming back to Aidensfield, angry at having been stood up.

Up in the abbey ruins, Bellamy was in a state of despair. When he finally made it back to Aidensfield, she was in a foul mood. Nevertheless, he took the plunge and popped the question. At first the answer seemed favourable but she later changed her mind. Craddock learned about the broken romance and returned Bellamy's letter of resignation. He may have lost the girl but at least he didn't have to sell double glazing.

## Jackie falls for a client

The rifts in the Bradleys' marriage had long been there for all to see. The latest bone of contention was starting a family. Mike felt that a baby might bring them closer together, whereas Jackie was too much of a career woman and was hugely relieved when Dr Summerbee told her that the result of her pregnancy test was

Mike and Bellamy became firm friends when sharing the police house.

out a troublesome customer. From that moment, Bellamy fell head over heels in love and hoped that Gina felt the same. Their first date got off to a bad start when she sang at a club and burst into tears, recalling her recent split with Andy Ryan. But she soon realised that her feelings for Bellamy were serious when an old flame of his briefly turned up in Aidensfield.

Gina's blossoming friendship with Bellamy did not escape the eagle eyes of Blaketon, who reminded him that a police officer was not allowed to marry a licensee. Craddock later

Mike's marriage finally disintegrated when Jackie fell for businessman Adrian Miller (right). She left Mike with nothing more than a goodbye note which he tore into pieces and cast to the wind high up on the moors.

negative. Jackie hadn't even told Mike that she could be pregnant. Unable or unwilling to confide in her husband, Jackie was an affair waiting to happen.

The catalyst for the eventual breakdown of the marriage was Adrian Miller, guest speaker at a

Celebrity Sightings – **Series Eleven**
**Freddie Jones** played the ageing art thief George Woodford; **Leslie Grantham** made a guest appearance as a Special Branch officer; **Clive Mantle** played the criminal cricketer Vinny Sanders; and **Jan Francis** appeared as Vivienne Keen, who accused Sergeant Merton of stealing her purse.

conference, whom Jackie defended on charges of assaulting a young woman in the hotel at which he was staying. The victim, Lisa, claimed that she'd had to fight off Adrian after he had insisted on having another drink in her room. Her blouse was torn and she had extensive bruising on her neck and arms.

For his part, Adrian denied having entered her room, saying that they had merely enjoyed a drink together at the hotel bar. Two wineglasses – one of them bearing Adrian's fingerprints – were found in Lisa's room, but Mike was unable to produce any witnesses until Humphrey, a guest at the hotel, called into the station to report that he had seen a man running from Lisa's room at the time of the alleged attack. He formally identified Adrian as the man in question.

Jackie was furious that Adrian had lied to her and demanded that he tell her the truth. He admitted having had a drink in Lisa's room but insisted that he hadn't attacked her. Mike's suspicions were aroused when he discovered that Lisa had given him a false home phone number. He checked the regional crime sheets and came up with a number of similar cases where wealthy men were accused of attacking young women. But Jackie thought the evidence against Adrian was overwhelming – that is, until Humphrey called Adrian to say that Lisa was willing to drop the case in return for £500. The police told Adrian to go along with the plan and arranged to watch Lisa and Humphrey collecting the payment before arresting the pair at a road block. A grateful Adrian expressed the hope that he might see Jackie again. She didn't say no.

Another prospective client of Jackie's was the auctioneer Giles Sutton, who was suspected of rigging cattle prices for the big buyers in return for a cut of the proceeds. Mike was investigating the allegations when he learned that a dinner with Jackie had been paid for by Sutton. Mike was furious, saying that he wasn't allowed to accept gifts, but Jackie did not want to offend a potentially valuable client.

The next morning Mike found an envelope containing £200 in his coat pocket and told Jackie that Sutton was trying to bribe him. Mike returned the cash to Sutton but Jackie said that he had no grounds to accuse Sutton of bribery and stormed off to her office. Sensing the fraught atmosphere between the couple, Bellamy suggested Mike take Jackie off on holiday somewhere. Checking his bank balance, he was pleasantly surprised and called on Jackie

to tell her the good news – and interrupted a meeting with Adrian Miller. No sooner had Mike paid the deposit on the holiday than he bumped into Sutton at an auction and confronted him about colluding with the main buyers. Sutton warned him off, mentioning his recent good fortune. A shocked Mike learned that £200 in cash had recently been paid into his bank account.

Jackie returned from lunch with Adrian to find an agitated Mike waiting for her. She merely confirmed his worst fears by telling him that he couldn't prove that he had returned the £200 to Sutton. Mike challenged Sutton about his trying to bribe a police officer but the auctioneer retaliated by producing a potentially incriminating photograph taken when Mike returned the money to him.

Mike was in deep trouble and received little sympathy from Craddock, who told him that he should have reported finding the cash and refused to allow Sutton to pay for an expensive dinner. Mike was suspended and warned that he could lose his job. Jackie angrily accused Craddock of failing to support her husband.

But there was an even bigger bombshell to come for Mike when Jackie told him that she was leaving him because she had fallen in love with Adrian. His only consolation was that he was quickly reinstated at work once CID revealed that they had been keeping tabs on Sutton. Indeed, Mike was even invited to take part in Sutton's arrest. But when he arrived home to tell Jackie he was off the hook, all he found was a farewell note. He went up to the moors to read it, tore it up in despair and tossed the scraps into the wind.

## A visitor for Vernon

When Saukas, a burly Lithuanian, turned up on Vernon's doorstep, Vernon was worried that he might be seeking retribution for a consignment of leaking umbrellas he once sold him. On the contrary, Saukas assured him he had made such a healthy profit on the umbrellas that he wished to discuss another business proposition – Lithuanian peat, an economical alternative to coal. Using his finest sales patter, Vernon soon shifted the peat, much to the disgust of Enoch, the local coalman.

However, nobody could get it to burn. Saukas maintained that it merely needed drying out and collected his share of the money while Blaketon and Gina, who had bought some of the peat, eventually resorted to igniting it with fire lighters. When Vernon and David saw thick smoke billowing from the Aidensfield Arms, they beat a hasty retreat.

Enoch, who had agreed to distribute the peat, was also being bombarded with angry customers, as a result of which Vernon sought out Saukas for an explanation. Saukas was vastly amused and admitted selling Vernon the useless peat in revenge for the faulty umbrellas. He refused to hand back the money until Vernon unnerved him by revealing that they had all been under surveillance from MI5. Saukas panicked and returned Vernon's money, together with a crate of vodka. For once it looked like Vernon might come out on top, but Vernon's celebrations were cut short when Enoch gave him a black eye for his trouble.

## The missing constables

Ashfordly police station welcomed a new young recruit in Tom Nicholson, transferred from Scarborough following an unfortunate incident with a donkey. He had unwittingly been party to a photograph that had appeared in the local newspaper of a donkey wearing his police helmet on Scarborough beach, giving rise to comments that the law was an ass. He soon found himself at the sharp end of police work when Lord Ashfordly announced that he was opening the hall to the public.

Despite a conspicuous police presence – well, Ventress – four sketches by John Constable were stolen from the hall library. The culprit, eighty-year-old George Woodford, tried to sell the sketches to a new fence, Collier, but the latter wasn't interested. Lord Ashfordly suspected his recently hired ticket seller, Eileen, of being involved and told her that her services were no longer needed. Eileen was George's housekeeper and was amused to find him hiding the stolen sketches behind a kitchen wall panel.

However, Craddock was far from amused to see a photograph in the *Gazette* of Ventress asleep on duty in the hall kitchen – even though Blaketon spotted from another photograph that the gathering that day had included George Woodford, an accomplished art thief. Nicholson was sent to bring George in for questioning, but arrived to find him gagged and tied up. As he started to remove George's gag, Nicholson was hit over the head by Collier. George revealed where he had hidden the sketches but, when Mike discovered they were missing, the old man collapsed under further questioning and died shortly afterwards. In his will, he left everything to Eileen.

At the funeral Ventress told Eileen that he thought George had been trying to protect her because he knew that she had moved the sketches from their original hiding place. Eileen admitted that she had transferred the sketches to the shed on George's allotment and also revealed that George had attempted to sell them to Collier. Ventress contacted Collier and arranged a meeting at Whitby Market on the pretext that he had some Georgian silver to sell. Nicholson identified Collier as his attacker and Collier incriminated himself when Ventress showed him one of the Constable sketches. He tried to run off but was apprehended by Mike.

## A fall from grace

Fleeing from Reynolds' Jewellers, a masked robber was knocked down by a car as he ran across the road to his getaway vehicle, a red Mini. The driver of the Mini, also masked, grabbed the jewellery and sped off, leaving his accomplice for dead. The injured robber was identified as Charlie Draper and he was placed under constant police guard as he lay in hospital. His first visitor was Jack Wetherby, an ex-con disguised as a doctor. He made a hasty exit when Bellamy told him that Draper was asleep. Bellamy later recognised Wetherby at the station as the bogus doctor, but Wetherby insisted that he had been at work at the time of the robbery. However, he changed his story when he was told that the getaway car had been found, along with plenty of forensic evidence, and admitted having stolen the car to order for Draper but he still denied that he had been part of the actual robbery.

Meanwhile, Blaketon was excited by the presence at the Aidensfield Arms of Vinny Sanders, a famous cricketer, and was hoping to persuade him to play in a pub match. Vinny's car was in for repairs at Scripps's garage, where the hapless David had developed an unfortunate knack of pouring diesel into petrol tanks, causing a

spate of breakdowns. After retrieving his repaired car from the garage, Vinny told Blaketon that he was retiring for the night. Over at the hospital, Nicholson fell asleep on duty and woke to find that Draper had vanished.

While road blocks were set up, Mike discovered that Vinny had been in prison for tax evasion at the same time as Draper and had been bankrupted by a huge tax bill. Investigating a noise outside the pub, Blaketon saw Vinny about to do a moonlight flit. Before he could remonstrate with him, Draper turned up and demanded his share of the jewellery. Draper collapsed in the ensuing struggle and Vinny drove off, hotly pursued by Blaketon. After a couple of miles, Vinny's car broke down thanks to David, allowing Blaketon to overhaul him. Vinny produced a gun and tried to hijack Blaketon's car, but Blaketon threw the car keys away.

When Bernie and David arrived on the scene moments later, Vinny commandeered their truck, only to be stopped at the next police road block and arrested. Bernie claimed that David was an unsung hero. And Craddock punished Nicholson by giving him two weeks' duty on a road crossing as a lollipop man.

## Changes afoot

While Mike was getting over Jackie's departure, passing his sergeant's exams and finding romance with Dr Tricia Summerbee, Craddock was patching up his marriage to Penny. Over dinner one evening, he told her that he had been promoted and was leaving the area, and she agreed to join him. His replacement, an ex-CID officer called Dennis Merton, would start a new chapter in the policing of Ashfordly and Aidensfield.

# chapter 9

# The Good, The Bad And The Ugly

### Lord Ashfordly

*(Rupert Vansittart)*

The owner of the stately home Ashfordly Hall, His Lordship is frequently beset by money problems, dishonest members of staff and visiting relatives. He recently fought to protect the family name after discovering that his grandfather had looted war trophies – including a severed head – from African natives in the nineteenth century.

### PC Phil Bellamy

*(Mark Jordon)*

Despite suffering from a distinct lack of ambition, the genial Bellamy is an asset to the Ashfordly force and displayed a growing maturity with the arrival of the naïve Nicholson, although he still enjoyed playing the occasional prank on the new boy. Acutely embarrassed by his grandmother, who used to bring gifts into the station, Bellamy has sometimes allowed police work to take second place to an active social life, which has seen him engaged twice but never quite make it up the aisle. He joined the police in the first place only because he thought girls would find the uniform irresistible. He was wrong. His love life remains choppier than the North Sea.

The ever-young Mike Bellamy, part of the original cast.

## Graham Blaketon

*(Dean Gatiss)*

Oscar Blaketon's teenage son by ex-wife Joan, Graham caused his father headaches by landing in trouble with the police over a drugs-related incident. Blaketon came down unnecessarily hard on the boy but subsequently tried to build bridges and was rewarded with a surprise visit from Graham one Christmas. However, it proved a false dawn and the pair have rarely met since.

## Oscar Blaketon

*(Derek Fowlds)*

The eyes and ears of Aidensfield, Blaketon went into the army before joining the police and carried the military planning and precision into his new job. Utterly pedantic and devoted to duty – traits that drove his wife to run off with the local butcher – Blaketon was forced to take early retirement after suffering a heart attack. His biggest regret was that he had never really been able to nail his arch-enemy, Greengrass. Blaketon briefly took over the running of the village post office, but was unable to settle, and, when he inherited money from an old aunt, he decided to buy the Aidensfield Arms.

Oscar Blaketon: the eyes and ears of Aidensfield.

A local councillor, he is a respected member of the community and, when he's not behind the bar of the pub, he can usually be found at the golf club, ready to pass on tips to his old friends at Ashfordly nick. However, he had no time for his successor, Craddock, and enjoyed undermining his authority at every available opportunity.

117

Maggie and Neil Bolton: an awkward reunion.

## Maggie Bolton

*(Kazia Pelka)*

District Nurse Maggie Bolton was a strong, forthright and independent woman, which was just as well considering the amount of heartache she suffered. After losing a baby, she split up with her doctor husband Neil, who then suddenly reappeared on the scene. At first the relationship between them was awkward but gradually she mellowed. However, no sooner had they got back together than he was killed in a fire, leaving her to bring up their baby Sam single-handed. There was a flicker of romance with PC Mike Bradley and then with a patient's son, Graham Rysinski, but in the end popular Maggie left Aidensfield to accept a hospital job.

## Dr Neil Bolton

*(David Michaels)*

The estranged husband of Maggie, Dr Neil Bolton, returned to the district to work at Ashfordly Hospital before becoming Aidensfield's GP – a job that should carry a health warning. Sure enough, he became the third incumbent in quick succession to die when he perished trying to rescue a youngster from a house fire. Just a few days earlier, Maggie had told him that she was pregnant.

## Jackie Bradley

*(Fiona Dolman)*

A solicitor, Jackie Lambert, as she was then known, arrived in Aidensfield to work for her Uncle Henry and immediately set about proving her worth. Her tough approach did not always endear her to the police, although it did eventually win the heart of Mike Bradley, whom she later married. But the union was never an easy one, and was not helped by the disapproval of her parents. As they argued more and more, she ran off with a former client, Adrian Miller, leaving Mike feeling bitter and betrayed.

## PC Mike Bradley

*(Jason Durr)*

Action man Mike Bradley breezed into Aidensfield from London on his motorbike and set about cleaning up the place. A conscientious upholder of the law – somewhat at odds with the long hair that he originally

sported – fearless Mike was quickly accepted into the village community, establishing a reputation for being firm but fair.

Friendships with several local women remained just that until he fell for – and married – feisty Jackie Lambert. Although they had more than their fair share of rows, he was devastated when she said she was leaving him and has only just started to trust women again. He was recently seen being comforted by Dr Tricia Summerbee.

## Sergeant Raymond Craddock

*(Philip Franks)*

Pompous, vain and with an inflated opinion of his own abilities, Craddock, a Welshman, ruled Ashfordly police station with ruthless efficiency. He revealed little about himself to his colleagues, thinking it a sign of weakness, and even kept quiet about his eccentric mother, Enid, an inveterate amateur sleuth. Neither did he socialise with his men, preferring to channel his extracurricular energies into ballroom-dancing competitions, where his stiffness and immaculate grooming made him something of a natural.

His wife Penny, being of a more human disposition, found him hard work and they drifted apart, only to be reunited when he

Mike Bradley: firm but fair.

119

accepted promotion away from Ashfordly. Craddock saw his long-overdue elevation as just another step towards his ultimate destiny: chief constable.

Raymond Craddock: put the boss into the bossa nova.

## Aunt Eileen
### (Anne Stallybrass)
Recently widowed herself, Kate Rowan's kindly Aunt Eileen lent a hand following her niece's death and helped Nick look after baby Katie. She became friendly with Blaketon – cooking supper for him and enjoying the odd round of golf – but eventually left the area to live in France with her wartime beau, Antonin.

## Dr Alex Ferrenby
### (Frank Middlemass)
A doctor of the old school, Alex Ferrenby was Kate Rowan's mentor and one of the reasons why she was happy to return to the area. As Aidensfield's GP, he was reluctant to move with the times, even after agreeing to take Kate on as a partner. He drowned in a fishing accident and was greatly mourned by the villagers.

## Claude Jeremiah Greengrass
### (Bill Maynard)
Accompanied everywhere by his flea-ridden lurcher Alfred, Greengrass was Aidensfield's most infamous country character, forever on the lookout for a way of making easy money. In Greengrass's case, 'easy' was invariably a euphemism for illegal. Operating out of his rundown smallholding, which he even tried to open to the public as a guest house at one point, he was the perpetrator of countless scams, the majority of which left him worse off financially than at the outset. With the exception of Blaketon, the local police tended to look benevolently upon his activities, issuing cautions rather than bringing charges. Greengrass thought he had struck it rich with a sale of land to the Ministry of Defence, only to be saddled with a hefty tax bill, which left him deeper in debt.

A local odd-job man who tried his hand at everything from gardening to training racehorses, Greengrass was joined in later years by the local funeral director, Bernie Scripps, and the hopeless David Stockwell. He eventually left Aidensfield to live in the Caribbean with his sister and help her spend the money she had won on the West Indies Sweepstake. For Greengrass, it was a welcome change of fortune. And the police weren't too sorry to see him go, either.

Claude Jeremiah Greengrass: likeable old rogue.

## Sergeant Dennis Merton
*(Duncan Bell)*
Craddock's successor as station sergeant, Merton did not exactly see Ashfordly as the posting of his dreams. Indeed, he was far from happy on arrival, having been demoted from CID following an infringement of regulations. For someone who was used to top-level investigations and nicking villains, his new role seemed to involve a lot of pen-pushing and community liaison.

## PC Tom Nicholson
*(Ryan Early)*
The bad publicity over his indiscretion with a donkey on Scarborough beach led the rookie PC Nicholson to be posted to the quieter climes of Ashfordly. Desperately eager to please, the ill-fated Nicholson was such a walking disaster area that some suspected his training film had starred the Keystone Kops. But, like a rubber ball, he bounced back from every setback, his confidence as high as ever.

Nicholson mistakenly saw himself as a real ladies' man, the best catch this side of Whitby cod. He thought he made girls' heads turn; in truth he made their stomachs turn.

### Did you know?
Nick Berry once claimed that he wasn't that interested in the musical side of his career. Despite this, he's had two top five single hits, recorded the theme tune to a top TV show and recently released an album. Not bad at all!

Kate and Nick Rowan: ill-fated love.

## Dr Kate Rowan

*(Niamh Cusack)*

Born not far from Aidensfield, Kate left the area to study medicine in London before landing a job at a leading hospital in the capital. However, the long hours put a strain on her marriage to Nick, as a result of which she selflessly agreed to his suggestion to move up to Yorkshire. In her role as Aidensfield's GP, she became a friend to many in the community and proved herself more than equal to the task of being a country doctor.

Despite the occasional tiff, she and Nick were very much in love, which made it all the more distressing when she died from leukaemia shortly after giving birth to their baby. In honour of his beloved wife, Nick named his new daughter Katie.

## PC Nick Rowan

*(Nick Berry)*

Following a turbulent youth that saw him in trouble for myriad minor misdemeanours, fresh-faced Nick decided to try to pass on the benefit of his wisdom to others by joining the Metropolitan Police. He envisaged himself as a friendly neighbourhood copper in the Dixon of Dock Green mould, but, with this becoming increasingly difficult in the changing London of the early sixties, he chose to return to North Yorkshire – where he had been evacuated as a boy during the war – to fulfil his ideal of community policing. He had met Kate in London but the pair settled in Aidensfield straight away, and his friendly approach made him many friends. Even Greengrass held a grudging respect for him.

Nick took Kate's death badly and for a while it looked as if he might go off the rails, but he found fresh happiness with the village schoolteacher, Jo Weston. Soon after marrying, the pair moved abroad, Nick having accepted a job with the Canadian police.

## Ruby Rowan

*(Diane Langton)*

Nick's widowed mother came up from London to help him through the aftermath of Kate's death but ruffled Gina's fathers by imposing her considerable will at the pub. Ever on the lookout for a man, Ruby briefly set her sights on Oscar Blaketon before

Ruby Rowan: Nick's brassy mother.

realising that he was a shade staid for her tastes. Nick later talked her out of allowing a bullying boyfriend, Ferdinand, to move in with her.

Bernie Scripps: the ferret-like funeral director.

## Bernie Scripps

*(Peter Benson)*

The funeral director with the hangdog expression, Bernie also runs the village garage. All too often he found himself involved in Greengrass's money-making schemes and no sooner had Claude gone abroad than Bernie's hopes of a peaceful life were shattered by the

123

unexpected arrival of his wayward half-brother Vernon, eager to stake his claim in the family business. Bernie's usual assistant is David Stockwell. No wonder he always looks so miserable.

## Vernon Scripps

*(Geoffrey Hughes)*

Vernon is a likable scallywag with a vaguely criminal past who not only took over Greengrass's house but also his territory. Never short of ideas but always short of the expertise to carry them out, Vernon quickly tried his hand at setting up a taxi firm, bottling spring water from source and setting up Aidensfield's first dating agency. Any day he expects to make his first million. He is currently just £999,999 short.

> ### Did you know?
> Niamh Cusack is not the only one to come from an illustrious acting family, Juliette Gruber's uncle was the late Walter Matthau – Juliette's parents are American, although Juliette moved to England when she was 12 months old.

Vernon Scripps: always on the make.

## David Stockwell

*(David Lonsdale)*

David Stockwell was living a lonely life in the woods with his mother when Greengrass took him under his wing and introduced him to the ways of the world. Still not exactly the sharpest tool in the box, David is a willing assistant to Bernie and accomplice to Vernon, but his innocence and gullibility lead him into all manner of scrapes. His heart is in the right place – it's just that nobody is too sure whether his brain is.

## Dr Tricia Summerbee

*(Clare Calbraith)*

After working as an intern at Ashfordly Hospital, young Tricia moved to the Aidensfield surgery to become the village's new GP. A competent and caring doctor, she soon became involved with the police on and off duty, attracting the attention of the newly liberated Mike Bradley.

David Stockwell: gullible and gormless.

the hope that he won't be noticed, although his encyclopaedic memory for past cases does occasionally come in useful. He smokes like a chimney – earning the nickname 'the Human Ashtray' – and has a penchant for eating hard-

## PC Alf Ventress

*(William Simons)*

Alf Ventress has made an art form of doing nothing. More couch potato than action man, he has made it his life's mission to avoid anything too stressful – a brief that encompasses all types of work. He even deliberately failed his eye test in the hope that he would be confined to desk duties and not have to venture outside.

His major attribute is his ability to fall asleep anywhere, any time, day and night. He likes to keep his head down at the station in

Alf Ventress: life in the bus lane.

boiled eggs. In the circumstances, it is little wonder that Mrs Ventress is happiest when he is working nights.

## George Ward
*(Stuart Golland)*

The former landlord of the Aidensfield Arms and uncle of Gina, George Ward had a natural mistrust of outsiders. Nevertheless, he took to Nick Rowan early on and began to trust him to the point where he would pass on the odd tip about something he had overheard. George was diagnosed as suffering from a rare disease of the immune system, which meant that he tired easily and he was eventually forced to retire from running the pub. He died not long afterwards.

## Gina Ward
*(Tricia Penrose)*

Rarely out of the courts in her native Liverpool, Gina avoided a prison sentence only on condition that she stay out of trouble by going to work for her Uncle George in Aidensfield. Fashion-conscious Gina arrived in her little bubble car at exactly the right moment – just as George needed an extra pair of hands to run the pub. Pretty and vivacious, she soon became a firm favourite with the male customers, but she brought with her a degree of Scouse nous and could handle herself in most situations.

When George stepped down, Gina became the licensee and currently works in tandem with the new owner, Oscar Blaketon. Over the years, she has pulled almost as many lads as she has pints, but she can also be a heartbreaker – as Bellamy found to his cost.

George Ward: fancy dress but no fancy ideas.

### Did you know?
Stuart Golland knew all about bar work when he started as the Aidensfield Arms landlord – he managed a bar for several years before becoming an actor.

Mrs Weston died of a cerebral haemorrhage before the nuptials and Jo felt guilty that the arguments had hastened her demise. Fortunately, her understanding father, Graham, was able to reassure her.

Gina Ward: pretty and vivacious.

## Jo Weston

*(Juliette Gruber)*

Arriving in Aidensfield as a new teacher at the village school, Jo soon found herself comforting Nick Rowan following the death of his wife. Although she lacked Kate's spirit, she did have a mind of her own and was not afraid to stand up for herself. She had plenty of practice when dealing with her mother, Fiona, who strongly disapproved of her forthcoming marriage to Nick.

> **Did you know?**
> Tricia Penrose used to sing in the pubs and clubs with her mum in their home town of Kirby. They called themselves Second Image.

Jo Weston: schoolteacher in love.

**EXECUTIVE PRODUCER**
Keith Richardson

## SERIES I
*Producer*
Stuart Doughty

*Writers*
Johnny Byrne
David Lane
Rob Gittins
Barry Woodward
Alan Whiting
Peter Barwood
Brian Finch

*Directors*
Roger Cheveley
Tim Dowd
Ken Horn
James Ormerod
Terry Iland

## SERIES II
*Producer*
Steve Lanning

*Writers*
Adele Rose
David Martin
David Lane
Jane Hollowood
Johnny Byrne
Brian Finch
Jonathan Critchley
Veronica Henry

*Directors*
Bob Mahoney
Ken Horn
Tim Dowd
Terry Marcel
Catherine Morshead

## SERIES III
*Producer*
Steve Lanning

*Writers*
David Martin
Brian Finch
Johnny Byrne
Michael Russell
Peter Palliser

*Directors*
Terry Marcel

Tim Dowd
Bob Mahoney
Catherine Morshead
Alan Grint

## SERIES IV
*Producer*
Martyn Auty

*Writers*
Michael Russell
Brian Finch
Jonathan Critchley
Johnny Byrne
Jane Hollowood
Veronica Henry
Lizzie Mickery
Steve Trafford
Freda Kelsall
Peter N. Walker

*Directors*
Ken Horn
Catherine Morshead
Baz Taylor
Tim Dowd
Matthew Evans

## SERIES V
*Producer*
Carol Wilks

*Writers*
Johnny Byrne
Lizzie Mickery
Jane Hollowood
Brian Finch
John Stevenson
Peter Tinniswood
Rob Gittins
Freda Kelsall
James Robson
Ron Rose
Jonathan Critchley

*Directors*
Alister Hallum
Tim Dowd
Tom Cotter
Ngozi Onwurah
David Innes Edwards
Graeme Harper
Gerry Mill
John Darnell

## SERIES VI
*Producer*
Gerry Mill

*Writers*
Brian Finch
Ron Rose
Jane Hollowood
David Lane
Johnny Byrne
Keith Temple
Peter Gibbs
Guy Meredith
Rob Gittins
Freda Kelsall

*Directors*
Tim Dowd
Ken Horn
James Hazeldine
Gwenann Sage
Michael Cocker
Gerry Mill
Graham Moore
Graham Wetherell
Tom Cotter

## Series VII
Producer:
Gerry Mill

*Writers*
Peter Gibbs
Brian Finch
Bill Lyons
Jane Hollowood
David Lane
James Stevenson
Susan Wilkins
Garry Lyons
Peter Barwood
Ron Rose
Veronica Henry
Carolyn Sally Jones
Jonathan Critchley

*Directors*
Ken Horn
Tom Cotter
Gerry Mill
Tim Dowd
Gerry Poulson
John Anderson
Garth Tucker
Brian Farnham
Sue Dunderdale

## SERIES VIII
*Producer*
Gerry Mill

*Writers*
Jane Hollowood
Brian Finch
Peter Gibbs
James Stevenson
Phil Ford
Tony Read
Michael Jenner
Helen Slavin
Peter Barwood
Susan Wilkins
Neil McKay
Rob Heyland
Johnny Byrne
Chris Thompson

*Directors*
Gerry Mill
Gerry Poulson
Brian Farnham
John Reardon
Garth Tucker
Terence Daw
Paul Walker
Frank W. Smith

## SERIES IX
*Producer*
Gerry Mill

*Writers*
Peter Gibbs
Johnny Byrne
Eric Deacon
Colin Shindler
Peter Barwood
Michael Jenner
John Flannagan and Andrew McCulloch
James Stevenson
Brian Finch
Gillian Richmond
Susan Wilkins
Neil McKay
Andrew McCulloch
Jane Hollowood

*Directors*
Gerry Mill
Gerry Poulson
Frank W. Smith
Roger Bamford
John Reardon

Paul Walker
Diana Patrick

## SERIES X
*Producer*
Gerry Mill

*Writer*
Peter Gibbs
Jane Hollowood
Neil McKay
Gil Brailey
Peter Barwood
Helen Blizard
John Milne
Michael Hall
Johnny Byrne
Gillian Richmond
Brian Finch
Susan Wilkins

*Directors*
Paul Walker
Gerry Mill
Gerry Poulson
Diana Patrick
Geoff Wonfor
Steve Goldie
Noreen Kershaw
Roger Bamford

## SERIES XI
*Producer*
Gerry Mill

*Writers*
Jane Hollowood
Johnny Byrne
Brian Finch
Peter Gibbs
John Flanagan and Andrew McCulloch
Douglas Watkinson
Jane McNulty
Jayne Hollinson
Paul Quiney
Jeff Dodds

*Directors*
Paul Walker
Noreen Kershaw
Jonas Grimas
Gerry Mill
Gerry Poulson
Diana Patrick
Roger Bamford
Bren Simson